DarkIsle

Dark Isle

D. A. NELSON

Delacorte Press

Published by Delacorte Press
an imprint of Random House Children's Books
a division of Random House, Inc.
New York

Originally published in the United Kingdom in 2007 by Strident Publishing Limited.

Visit us on the Web! www.randomhouse.com/kids

Educators and librarians, for a variety of teaching tools, visit us at
www.randomhouse.com/teachers

Library of Congress Cataloging-in-Publication Data
Nelson, D. A.
DarkIsle / D. A. Nelson.—1st American ed.
p. cm.
Summary: Helped to escape from her evil guardians and a life of drudgery by a dodo
and a rat, ten-year-old Morag joins her new companions on a dangerous and difficult
mission involving a stone dragon, the stolen Eye of Lornish that guards the magical
land of Marnoch Mor, and her own unfulfilled destiny and mysterious past.
ISBN 978-0-385-73630-5 (hardcover)—ISBN 978-0-385-90600-5 (Gibraltar lib. bdg.)
[1. Orphans—Fiction. 2. Dragons—Fiction. 3. Animals—Fiction. 4. Fantasy.] I. Title.
PZ7.N43377Dar 2008
[Fic]—dc22
2007045775

The text of this book is set in 13.5-point Fournier Regular.

Book design by Angela Carlino

Printed in the United States of America

10 9 8 7 6 5 4 3 2 1

First American Edition

for
Ian, Emma, Xander and Robbie
xxx

WITH THANKS TO:

Ian, for his never-ending support;

Natalie, for being my first reader;

Jonathan, for his encouragement;

my dad, for his editing skills;

my mum, for her enthusiasm;

the rest of the family and all my friends;

Alison McAllister and Melanie West at North

Ayrshire Council for all their help and ideas;

and Keith, Graham and Alison at Strident

for taking a chance on me.

1

The dragon stared out over a menacing gray sea, the dark waters swelling below the raggedness of three miles of sandy hilltops that had been her home these past thirty years. An angry black sky warned of a storm brewing, and the dragon shivered at the thought of enduring yet another winter. She had seen many such squalls lying there on the hill overlooking Irvine Beach, but this one was going to be a beauty. The clouds sagged, heavy with rain, and it looked like it would only be a matter of time before the sky opened up and a tempest rained down on her. She worried that the bricks of her body would not hold up to this latest squall; after all this time she was feeling old and worn out. The wind lashed against her cold stone flanks, whipping sand into her unblinking eyes. Oh, what she would give to be real again; to stretch her stiff and aching legs, to rise up again. To be free.

And so it began to rain. Cold, harsh raindrops fell like tiny arrows against the dragon's unmoving stone hide. She braced herself against the terrible weather that was to come, forever alone and miserable.

⁓❦⁓

A few miles down the coast in a ramshackle guesthouse overlooking a large sewage pipe on the beach, a small ten-year-old girl was watching the approaching storm from the window of her attic bedroom. A solitary, sad little figure, the girl often knelt up against the headboard of her bed beneath the window and gazed out the dirty glass. She liked being up here, hidden from view where no one could see her. She could forget who she really was and fantasize about the lives of the people who often walked by.

In the summer, she would watch as the shiny cars filed into the empty field nearby, turning it into a makeshift car park. The car doors would burst open and out would spill excited children running with spades and balls toward the sea. They were always on the beach before anyone else, daring each other to go into the cold water first. Their parents brought up the rear, laden down with striped umbrellas and wicker picnic baskets, multicolored sun hats and sun cream. From her vantage point, Morag (for that was the girl's name) saw everything. There was the joy radiating from the children, the togetherness of their parents and the love of the family. How she wanted to be one of those children getting hugs and kisses from a mother or father. How she yearned for a family of her very own.

The beach was hardly used in winter. Only dog walkers braved the cold, cold sea air, their faces set hard against the stinging wind and salty spray, the fur of their dogs dancing wildly in the gale. Morag loved to watch the dogs; she had always wanted a dog to look after and love, but Jermy and Moira wouldn't allow it. They're too dirty, they said. Costs money, they said.

She sighed long and hard. There were no dogs or holidaymakers playing on the sand on this wild October morning. The beach was deserted. There weren't even any sea birds trotting along the shoreline. Morag turned away from the window and got down from her bed. She supposed she'd better start her chores before breakfast. She didn't want to get locked in the cellar again.

Her foster parents, Moira and Jermy Stoker, were still snoring loudly in their bedroom on the floor below. She could hear them above the rumbling of the storm, snorting and snuffling away in their bed, oblivious to the gale outside. Thunder grumbled over the little house, rain lashed at the windows, and the wind tugged at the doors and shutters. Morag shivered. There was no central heating in the house and it was freezing. Barefoot and wearing her too-small pajamas and frayed pink housecoat, she grabbed hold of her special book and stuffed it into one of her pockets. This was all she had left of her real parents. It was a red leather-bound book of ancient poetry, about the size of a prayer book, and inside on the first page was the inscription that made her heart sing every time she read it. They were simple words, but they meant a lot to her:

To Morag,
Until we meet again . . .
Lots of love, Mum and Dad xxx.

There was a marker tucked away on page thirteen, held tight against a short poem. It was a little piece of pink cardboard, just big enough to sit snugly in the palm of her hand. It appeared to be an old-fashioned train ticket, and marked on it, in faded black letters, was the name of a station that, despite her best efforts, Morag had never been able to decipher. There was an *M* and an *r*, but she couldn't read the rest.

The book felt reassuringly weighty in her housecoat pocket as she slipped out of her room and crept out of the attic and down the creaking, cracking stairs to the kitchen, where she could get warm beside the stove.

Stoker's Seaview Guesthouse was always really creepy in the morning, and Morag hated being the first one up. The house was dark and shadowy on the brightest of days, and every room was in desperate need of some care and attention. Neglected paint peeled off the woodwork, strips of wallpaper were missing in patches from the walls, and the carpets were stained and threadbare. There were six rooms in the tall narrow house near the beach, not counting Morag's bedroom in the attic. On the ground floor was a living room full of burst sofas and chairs, a dining room with no furniture in it other than Jermy's locked desk with its computer, and a large, dirty kitchen that was dominated by an old stove. One of the three unloved bedrooms on the first floor was Jermy and Moira's untidy room and the other two were permanently unwanted and unopened guest bedrooms. Morag often asked if she could move down to one of the proper bedrooms, but Jermy and Moira always refused, telling her the rooms were needed for guests. But no one ever came.

"Besides," Jermy would say with a sneer. "You're better up in the attic out of our way."

Morag's feet were freezing by the time she reached the kitchen. It didn't help that the floor was covered with torn linoleum that was always icy underfoot, even in summer. She wished she had put her socks on before she had come down, but it was too late to run back upstairs—*those two* might hear her go past as she went up, and she didn't want to wake them. She tiptoed over to the kitchen table and dragged one of the rickety chairs over to the stove. Quietly, she sat down and savored the lovely heat coming from it. Lifting both feet, she placed them within an inch of the old cooker's body. Ah, that was better. The stove never went off, as she made sure it was well stocked with driftwood, and its flaking red body was always hot: too hot to touch, but just perfect to be near. She felt its heat slowly restore the feeling to her numb feet. It was bliss.

Although the house could be cold and creepy, this was the only time of the day when Morag felt she had it completely to herself. With Jermy and Moira still in bed, she had time to daydream about what life would be like if she was a princess or a famous film star, or just someone else's child. She thought about the pair upstairs, her parents, or so they called themselves. They weren't really her parents—they had adopted her when she was a baby—but they liked to pretend they were. They didn't act like real parents; there were no hugs, no kisses and certainly no love. There was only their coldness and anger. Jermy usually ignored her, and Moira just screamed orders and accusations at her. And then there were all the things they expected her to do around the guesthouse: the dusting and wiping and scrubbing and ironing and washing and shopping and cooking. Most of the time she wished she had a different life, or at least a different mum and dad. She couldn't remember her real parents and didn't know what had happened to them. Jermy had said they had run away and abandoned her, but Morag didn't believe that for a minute. They were lost, she told herself, and one day they would find her again, she was positive of that.

Her stomach rumbled, reminding her that she hadn't eaten since yesterday teatime. She glanced at the clock above the sink. It was nearly seven o'clock. She just had time to eat a jam sandwich before she had to start the day's round of chores. The dishes were still piled high in the sink, the pots and pans encrusted with the burnt debris of last night's dinner. It would take forever to get through them. And she still had to start Jermy and Moira's breakfast. She sighed.

Suddenly a snarling voice jolted her to attention.

"What's to eat, you lazy brat?"

Morag jumped. She spun around. There was Moira in all her glory, swaying slightly in the doorway. Although Moira's hair started off ash gray at the scalp, it was mostly flaming red and in such disarray that it looked like an abandoned bird's nest. More like an abandoned bird's nest *on fire*. Morag smiled to herself. Here and there, rollers dangled from stray crimson wisps like corks on bits of string. "Argh! What's this?" Moira suddenly shrieked, tugging at one with her stubby fingers. It wasn't a roller—it was a small foil-covered chocolate roll she'd used by mistake. She raised her badly drawn eyebrows, cracking her thick coating of white makeup. *Her eyebrows are almost the same size this morning*, Morag thought, *but she ought to stop drawing round a cup with a marker pen to make them*.

"I suppose I'll have to have *this* until you eventually get that frying pan going!" she said, wagging the chocolate roll at Morag.

Under Moira's tatty white nightdress, the one singed with burns, were her clothes from the night before: a dress covered in violent green, brown and black swirls and a necklace that looked like a grinning row of dog's teeth. She lifted her smoldering cigar to her lips and blew the bitter-smelling smoke out through her nostrils. From where she was sitting, Morag started to cough and waved it away.

"Well?" Moira hiccupped. She and Jermy hadn't got in until four that morning. At least, that was the time on Morag's electric alarm clock when she had glanced at it after being woken up by them crashing through the front door.

"Sorry, Moira," said Morag as she jumped up. "I didn't think you would want breakfast this early. I thought you might like a lie in." She walked over to the cupboard where the food was kept, and began to root inside for the cooking fat.

"Well, you're not here to think. Leave that to me! While we're at it, I think you should be calling me Mum," Moira drawled. She took a drag of her cigar. "Is that too much to ask? 'Mum.' Is it such a hard word to say?" She stumbled over to the little wooden table and clumsily threw herself down on a chair. "Eh? Is it?"

Morag looked up at her, this cruel, lazy woman. She *wasn't* her mother and never would be. No one deserved to have Moira as a mother. Morag knew it would only be a matter of time before her real mother came to take her away. And when she told her how badly she had been treated, Jermy and Moira would be in serious trouble. They might even go to jail. This was a thought that often comforted her, and made life more bearable, but she didn't dare show it.

"No . . . . Moir—I mean, *Mum,*" she said meekly. She knew better than to rile Moira, whose temper would be worse this morning after her late night and lack of sleep. Morag reached into the fridge and pulled out the cold wet bacon, the lumpy greasy sausages and a few feather-covered eggs. But when she opened another cupboard, which housed plates and bowls, her heart sank. There were no clean ones left. She looked at the sink and then at Moira, who had been watching her intently. Realization quickly dawned on Moira's face. Her thickly powdered brow furrowed. Her little piggy eyes darkened. Her ragged pink-smeared lips curled into a snarl to reveal brownish teeth. Morag shuddered and took a step back.

"Did you go to bed last night without doing the washing up?" Moira growled. "Weren't you always told that your chores had to be finished before you could go to bed? You spoilt, good-for-nothing girl!"

"I didn't have time, Moira—I mean, Mum," pleaded Morag, suddenly feeling very sick.

"Didn't have *time*?" Moira scoffed. "Oh, it must be hard to fit us in when you've got so many friends to entertain— no, wait. You don't have any friends, remember?" she screeched. She stood up and stomped over to Morag, who was cowering beside the cupboard. She bent down so that they were nose to nose. Her breath was so overpowering that Morag turned away in disgust.

"So what were you doing all last night when you weren't doing your work?" Moira demanded. "You couldn't have been playing with anyone." She snorted. "I don't know how many times I've told Jermy you're a useless lump. Your parents must've thought the same or they wouldn't have left you behind. I bet you were having a good laugh at us, weren't you? Bet you thought it was funny to leave the mess."

"No, no, I wasn't, honestly." Morag took a step back from her. "I finished the rest of the jobs and then I had to do my homework and I was going to do the dishes, but I fell asleep on my bed. I'm sorry! Look, I'm doing them right now," she said, terrified of what might happen next. Unconsciously, her hand felt for the comforting form of the book in her pocket and she held it as she willed Moira not to get any angrier.

"Too right, you are," screamed Moira. "But not until you've made my breakfast. And hurry up, I'm starving."

She took another draw of her cigar and blew the smoke at Morag as if this would make the girl work harder.

"What's all the racket?" The stern face of Jermy appeared at the door. Tufts of his greasy hair stuck up at strange angles, as if he had received a massive electric shock. "Can't a man get a decent night's kip without you screaming like a banshee, woman?" he barked.

"She," said Moira, pointing a podgy finger at Morag, "didn't finish the housework last night." She folded her arms in front of her chest, a look of vile smugness on her face.

"What do you mean she *didn't* finish them?" roared Jermy with a sneer, looking around. He spied the dirty dishes in the sink and strode forward, a menacing frown etched on his haggard face. Morag's heart started to race. She knew what was coming next. Jermy crouched right in front of her, his blotchy angular face just a couple of inches from her nose. She shrank back, screwed her eyes closed and held her breath.

"Get. Them. Done," he snarled deliberately. "Or you'll get a piece of what for, you hear?" He was so close that she could feel the spit flying from his lips. "Look at me! Do you hear me?" His gruff voice was scarier than normal.

Morag peeked from under her eyelids and nodded dumbly.

"But get my breakfast first!" piped Moira from the corner. She had returned to sit at the table. "Tell her, Jermy."

Jermy rolled his bloodshot eyes and stood. "And get the fry-up ready for your mother." He lowered his hand and then turned his back on her. Relieved, Morag felt she could breathe again. She watched as Jermy walked away from her to join Moira at the table. She looked at them both, her heart once more filling with fear.

"She's not my mother," she said quietly through trembling lips. Her words stopped Jermy in his tracks and he spun around, eyes glinting with malice.

"What did you say?" he demanded. Once again, he strutted toward Morag, his eyes narrowed, like a cat stalking its prey.

Morag was terrified. Her heart thumped wildly in her chest now, and she began to wish she had kept her mouth shut. But she still told him again. "I said she's not my mother." She even managed to speak more steadily than before.

"Not your mother? Of course Moira's your mother— she's the only mother you'll ever have!" screamed Jermy. "Your own mother didn't want you. She gave up on you when she knew what she was in for. No wonder your mum and dad ran off. They couldn't stomach being saddled with you. If it wasn't for us you'd be dead. We've given you everything—a good home, food in the fridge, a roof over your head—and this is how you repay us! You're an ungrateful little good-for-nothing!" His face was purple with rage.

"She's a disgrace, Jermy," goaded Moira from her corner as she emptied the previous day's cigar ash into a half-full mug of cold tea.

Morag said nothing. She knew there was no point, as it would only make matters worse. She waited for Jermy to punish her, but something odd happened. Instead of threatening her again, he just gave up. His face relaxed; he sighed and turned away.

"Oh, what's the use?" he said. "Just get on and make Moira her breakfast. And get me a cup of tea. Right now. I need one after last night." He walked away from the little girl and grabbed the chair which, up until five minutes ago, Morag herself had been sitting on. He dragged it over to the table and sat down beside his wife.

"I told you we should have taken her to an orphanage and changed her for a boy," he told Moira more quietly. "A boy would have been much better than that little madam. They're stronger, more reliable. She's totally useless. You can see now why they left her behind."

"Do you blame them?" laughed Moira. "If we weren't so nice, Jermy my love, we'd have abandoned her as well. Just look at her."

Usually, when Jermy and Moira were having a go at her, Morag would do her best to ignore them, blinking away the tears, but for some reason she couldn't let the matter drop. Maybe it was the way Jermy was being so casually horrible about her parents, or maybe it was the way he was speaking about *her;* she didn't know, but something welled up inside of her, a kind of anger that just wouldn't go away no matter how hard she tried to suppress it. It bubbled up like lava under a volcano and then exploded, showering the startled Jermy and Moira with sparks.

"My parents didn't abandon me!" Morag yelled, lifting a plate from the sink. "They didn't mean to leave me." She smashed it off the sink, breaking it into a hundred little pieces. "My parents did love me!" she shrieked as big fat tears began to roll down her face. She threw a glass at the startled couple. They ducked and it smashed off the wall. "They didn't abandon me, they got lost. Okay? They're lost!"

Crash! Another plate followed the glass and it, too, smashed off the wall. Stale wine and last night's dinner slid down the paintwork. "And you two are not my mum and dad and never will be!" She sobbed.

"That's *it!*" Jermy roared from under the table, where he and Moira had taken refuge. He peeked up just as Morag lifted a large soup pot above her head.

"You've done it now! Hoi, put that down! Put it down!"

Crash! It clanged off the table and bounced onto the floor close to Jermy's knee. Smiling wickedly, he grabbed it and, placing it carefully on his head as protection, he stood up. Yesterday's cold soup ran down his bony face, but he ignored it as he edged forward toward Morag.

"Go get her, Jermy!" shouted Moira from under the

table. Smash! Morag began to quicken her assault. She grabbed whatever she could find and threw it all at the advancing Jermy: plates, forks, glasses, cups and saucers. Jermy swatted them away one by one with his big hands and kept coming. Within seconds he was upon her and had grabbed hold of both her arms. She struggled to get free, but he was too strong for her. She tried to kick him, but he moved out of the way and held her there until she had tired herself out and couldn't struggle or kick any more. He put his arms around her and pinned her to his chest. She was trapped.

"That'll do," he snarled into her ear. "Gotcha! You're in for it now! Into the cellar with you, with the rats and the ghosts!"

"No! NO!" shrieked Morag as he dragged her to the door. "I'm sorry! I'm sorry!" Morag dreaded the cellar the most. It was dark, it was damp, it was really creepy, and there was only one way in and one way out—through the door in the kitchen. She was sure it was haunted, as there were always strange noises coming from down there.

Once he had hold of her, it was only too easy for Jermy to drag her squealing to the cellar door. Although he was a thin beanpole of a man, he was quite strong and didn't have any trouble lifting her to her punishment.

"No! No!" screamed Morag. "Don't put me in there! Please, Jermy, I'll behave, I promise."

"Open the door, Moira," he ordered, taking no heed of Morag's pathetic pleas nor her efforts to kick him. "She stays there until she calms down."

"Good riddance to bad rubbish," said Moira as she swiftly got up and unlocked the cellar door. She held it open while Jermy threw the struggling child inside. Morag stumbled as she was thrown forward and fell to her knees on the landing—the only thing that prevented her from tumbling down the steep stairs into the deep cavern of the cellar below. When she got to her feet, the door was closing behind her, sealing her into the cold darkness. She hammered on the hard wood with her fists and rattled the handle loudly.

"Let me out!" she cried. "Let me out!"

She stopped to listen for movement outside.

"Shut up! No one's going to let you out!" Jermy's voice was muffled behind the door.

"Please let me out!" she begged. "I'll be good, I promise!"

She heard them laughing.

"Too late for that!" spat Moira.

"Let me out!" Morag cried again, and began to bang on the door even more loudly. "Let me out!"

But her cries fell on deaf ears. Jermy and Moira were either ignoring her or they were no longer in the kitchen, for they did not reply to her screams. Morag continued battering on the door until she was exhausted and had to stop. Her arms ached and her throat was sore as she slumped down in the dark. She realized it was no use. They weren't going to let her out—not yet, anyway. She sat against the wall and looked around fearfully. By now her eyes had adjusted to the dark and she could make out the top two steps disappearing into the cellar. A freezing cold breath of air rushed up the stairs and brushed against her face, and in the cellar below a slight rustling could be heard.

Alone in the dark, Morag whimpered quietly and wondered what was waiting for her down there.

2

Morag did not know how long she had been in the cellar nor when she had fallen asleep, but she was stiff and sore and very cold when she finally woke up. She looked around her in confusion and suddenly remembered where she was and how she had come to be there. Fear gripped her again and her heart began to quicken. She shifted slightly to ease the numbness of her body and felt something hard under her leg. Carefully putting her hand down, scared she might touch a rat or a creepy crawly, her fingers closed around a long, heavy object. She gripped it tightly. It felt like a flashlight. She felt along its hard body. It *was* a flashlight. She lifted it up and found the switch. With hope in her heart, her fingers clumsy and numb with the cold, she turned it on. The flashlight blinked to life with a bright beam of light. It's working! she thought, and sighed with relief. At least now with a bit of light she didn't feel quite so frightened in this cold, dank prison. She swung the flashlight around; its light picked out the cracks in the gray stone walls and illuminated a few more of the simple wooden steps and the banister that led down to the cellar floor. She looked at them uneasily. She was in a dilemma. Now she had the flashlight she could see where she was going and could negotiate the stairs to the bottom to switch on the main light. This would banish the darkness for good and she would be able to see what she was doing. However, there was just one thing wrong with this plan: she was too frightened to go down the stairs by herself. There could be monsters or ghosts or worse down there. She weighed the risks. Firstly, she had no idea how much longer she would be imprisoned. Secondly, having had no breakfast or lunch—she supposed it was past lunchtime by now—she was growing hungrier and colder. She remembered Moira saying there were jars of pickles and fruit kept down there and if she could get down she could open one and eat the contents. Jermy and Moira would never know. Thirdly, there might be old clothes or shoes she could wear to keep herself warm. She looked down the stairs again, scared of what might be waiting for her there. Morag, you are just being silly, she told herself crossly. There is nothing down there except some jars of food and some rubbish. It is only a cellar, after all.

With a big exhalation of breath, she rose to her feet.

Her heart sped up a little and her throat constricted into a tight knot.

"Okay, Morag," she said aloud to sound braver than she was actually feeling and just in case she was not alone. Her words echoed off the walls and were swallowed up in the darkness. "It'll only take two minutes to run down the stairs and flick that light switch. Then you'll be able to see that there's absolutely *nothing* to be afraid of," she tried to assure herself. "Right," she said. "After three: one . . . two . . ."

"Three!" finished another voice. There was the sound of shushing. Morag nearly fainted on the spot. She sat back down on the landing.

"Who's that?" she called with a tremor in her voice, swinging the flashlight into the darkness below her. "Who's there?"

"Oh, no one," replied a singsong voice. "You must be dreaming!"

"Shhh," said another voice crossly. "She'll hear you."

"But I want her to hear me, how else will she think she's dreaming if I don't tell her?" the first voice said matter-of-factly.

"Will you shush?" rasped the second voice in a loud whisper. "Oh, what's the point? It's too late now anyway. Thanks to you she knows we're here."

"I'm sorry, Bertie, I really am."

"Shhh!"

"I didn't mean to—"

"Shhhh!"

Sigh. "Okay, I'll be quiet."

"Oh, for goodness' sake!" the voice called Bertie said crossly.

"Who's down there?" called Morag, who was beginning to feel very frightened now. "Are you ghosts? Because if you are, I don't mind. Just let me out, will you? I won't tell anyone I've seen you, I promise." And with that she began to cry quietly and tried the door handle again. Rattle, rattle, rattle. The door was well and truly locked. There was no way out for her.

"Now look what you've done!" said Bertie. "You've gone and frightened her."

"Sorry, miss," said the other voice. "I didn't mean to frighten you."

"Who are you?" Morag began to sob. "What do you want?" She was sure they were ghosts who had come to get her. Suddenly there was a footstep on the staircase. "Stay right where you are!" she shouted. "I've got a gun!" she lied.

Another stair creaked as whoever was coming up took another step. She swung the flashlight's beam down the stairs, but could see no one there, only darkness.

"What do you want?" she cried. "Please leave me alone. I'm just a girl who's been locked in the cellar. Please don't hurt me!"

"We're not here to hurt you," said the voice called Bertie, sounding kindlier than before. "I'm just coming up to say hello now that thanks to Aldiss you know we're here. Honestly, Aldiss, you can be such an idiot. I said you had to be quiet, didn't I?"

"Sorry, Bertie."

The sound of slow footsteps got closer as Morag peered into the darkness.

"Are you—are you sure you're not going to hurt me?" she stammered nervously. She still couldn't see anyone, when suddenly, into the light stepped something. Wait, she thought, what is this? Clawed feet, gray feathers and a hooked beak. Morag was puzzled, as she was sure she had only seen one of these creatures in books. Surely it couldn't be, she thought. It couldn't be? A dodo wearing a little satchel leapt elegantly up the stairs and landed at Morag's feet with a flourish of its tiny wings. She stared at it in astonishment.

"Albert Alonzo Fluke, at your service, miss," he said with a small bow. "Bertie to my friends," he added with a wink.

"P-p-leased to m-m-meet you," she said with a stutter. "I—I'm Morag." She couldn't take her eyes off the little fat gray bird. "But you're a . . ."

"Dodo? Yes, that's correct," said Bertie.

"But aren't you supposed to be—?"

"Extinct? Yes! Well, no, not really. We pretend to be extinct. We moved, actually," he said proudly.

"You moved?" repeated Morag. She was finding it hard to believe there was a real live dodo standing before her. And furthermore, a real live dodo that could talk!

"Too many humans took over our island and it became rather overcrowded. We have a nice place now, though," he assured her, "which is much better."

"I see."

Just then there came the sound of huffing and puffing and a small brown rat appeared at Bertie's back. Morag shifted back a bit as she didn't like rats.

"Is he with you?" began Morag.

"Aldiss G. Drinkwater," the rat said breathlessly. He was the owner of the other voice.

"*G*?" asked Morag.

"Stands for 'Great'," he said proudly.

"If only." Bertie sneered. "Tell her what it really stands for."

The rat looked a little crestfallen, and seemed embarrassed. "Graham," he said miserably.

"I think that's a lovely middle name," Morag assured him.

"You do?" His little bright eyes sparkled. Bertie snorted with laughter.

"Of course I do . . . um . . . Sorry, what was your first name?" It was Morag's turn to feel embarrassed.

"Aldiss," said the rat.

"Aldiss," repeated Morag. She repeated the name in her head so that she wouldn't forget it again.

Morag suddenly remembered her manners. "Nice to meet you . . . er . . . Bertie and Aldiss," she said with wonder. I must be dreaming right enough, she thought, because dodos don't exist and rats can't talk. She pinched her right arm just to make sure, having read somewhere that this is what you should do if you thought you were still asleep and dreaming. "Ow!" she cried. She was definitely awake, as her arm ached.

"What? What is it?" Aldiss asked, startled and glancing around nervously. "What's happened?"

Bertie sighed and ruffled his feathers. "She pinched herself to make sure she's not dreaming," he explained. "Isn't that right, Morag?"

Morag was now glad of the darkness because it meant they couldn't see how red her face had turned. "It's just that, well, dumb animals aren't *supposed* to talk."

"Dumb animals?" cried Aldiss. "*Dumb* animals? Who are you calling dumb? I'll have you know that I am a rat! And rats are very intelligent. How dare you call us dumb!"

"I didn't mean to! Oh, what's the use!" She sighed. This was turning out to be a very strange afternoon. "I only meant that I've never heard an animal, I mean a rat, or . . . or . . . even a dodo talk before. It's all new and strange to me."

"Have you ever *tried* to start a conversation with a rat or a dodo before?" Bertie asked patiently.

"Well, no, I haven't. But then I've never actually met a rat or a dodo before," she replied. Not a live rat anyway, she thought, remembering the dead ones she had seen caught in Jermy's many traps around the house.

"Well, there you are, then," said Bertie triumphantly.

"Yes, there you are, then," repeated Aldiss a little huffily.

There was an awkward silence and then everyone tried to talk at once.

"So what are you doing . . . ?" began Morag.

"I see you're locked . . . ," said Bertie.

23

"Did you know there was cheese . . . ?" Aldiss started to say.

"In the cellar!" they said together, and laughed. "Ladies first," said Bertie.

"Well," Morag started. "I wanted to ask what you two were doing in Jermy and Moira's cellar."

"Ah, we came up in the wrong place," explained Bertie, throwing Aldiss a meaningful look. "*Someone* misread the underground map and *someone* said we should turn right when in fact we ought to have gone on for a bit more and turned left! Isn't that right, Aldiss?"

The rat hung his little whiskered head in shame. "I've never read an underground map before," he said.

"Aldiss," said Bertie patiently. "You were reading it upside down."

"Was I?" Aldiss scratched his head, puzzled. "You should have told me."

"I didn't realize until . . ." Bertie trailed off. "Oh, never mind, it's done now." He turned to Morag. "So why are you here, locked in this cellar?"

"Are you a prisoner?" asked Aldiss wide-eyed with curiosity, as he had never met a prisoner before.

"Sort of," replied Morag. "Jermy and Moira locked me down here because they think I've been bad."

" *Been bad*'? What did you do?" Aldiss asked. He suddenly thought of something. "Are you dangerous?" he asked a little fearfully, and moved to hide behind Bertie.

"No." Morag smiled and explained what had happened and about her horrible life with Jermy and Moira, how her parents had abandoned her and how Jermy and Moira didn't want her to see other children.

"They even tried to stop me going to school," she added. "But the old lady who lived in the house just up the beach from us called the police and they made Jermy and Moira take me."

"What happened then?" asked Aldiss.

"Jermy set the old lady's house on fire and the Fire Brigade had to rescue her. She ended up going into a home," replied Morag. "I couldn't tell anyone because Jermy threatened to 'knock my block off' if I did."

"What a terrible pair!" said Bertie.

"I know," said Morag miserably, suddenly feeling very sad. "Anyway, they are the only family I have, so I suppose I'll have to put up with them until I'm old enough to get a job and a house of my own. Then I won't have to have anything more to do with them." A tear welled in her eye. "But I wish my real mum and dad were here."

"What happened to them?" asked Bertie, gently stroking her arm with one of his little gray wings.

"I don't know. They disappeared without a trace and left me behind in the boardinghouse," she said, and looked at the ground. "All I have left of them is a book of poetry," she added, bringing it out. She opened it on her lap, at the page where her parents had stopped reading, and had marked their place with a train ticket. "I have nothing else. I don't even have a photograph of them so that I can see what they looked like."

They all fell silent for a minute. Then Aldiss suddenly became very excited.

"Why don't you run away?" he squeaked.

"To where?" said Morag. "I have no money, no friends and nowhere to run away to."

"Why not come with us!" cried Aldiss, jumping up and down. "We're on a mission. We could do with a Big Person like you."

Morag's eyes lit up. "A mission? Really? Could I come with you?" She liked the idea of an adventure, as anything was better than living with Jermy and Moira.

"Yes! We'll go together on a big adventure and we'll—"

"Aldiss!" interrupted Bertie sharply, making the rat jump in fright. "She can't come with us and you know why."

"She'd be perfect!"

"No, Aldiss, it's not possible." He turned to Morag. "I'm sorry, but our mission is just too dangerous for the likes of you."

It was Morag's turn to be crestfallen. For a moment it had seemed like her life was just about to get better.

"S'okay," she said. "I understand." She pulled her knees up and put her head down. "I'll just stay here and wait until Jermy and Moira decide to let me out, whenever that will be. Don't worry, I promise I won't say anything about seeing the two of you."

Bertie studied her closely. "I tell you what." He sighed. Morag looked up hopefully. "If you promise to keep quiet about us we'll help you escape from here, but after that you're on your own."

"Oh, thank you! That would be more than enough!"

she cried, clapping her hands in delight and nearly dropping the flashlight.

"But that's all, remember," continued Bertie seriously.
"After that Aldiss and I must continue our mission and you
must go and do whatever it is you humans do." He held out
a wing. "Do we have a deal?"

Morag took the wing and shook it. "We certainly do,"
she said, smiling.

Then with a tink, the flashlight went out.

"Drat!" she said. "The battery must be dead."

"How are we going to find the tunnel now?" squealed
Aldiss, his voice a little shaky.

"There's a light switch at the bottom of the stairs," said
Morag, who suddenly felt very confident and put it down
to the company of her new friends. "Come on," she said,
"let's go and find our way out of here."

3

It had been a long time since Morag had seen the cellar with the light on and it hadn't changed a bit. Once she had found the switch, she could see there was nothing to be afraid of down there. Lit by a single dusty old bulb, the cellar was as gloomy and damp as she remembered, but not nearly as scary. The dodo and the rat looked around in wonder at the junk littering the floor.

"Wow!" said Aldiss, his little black eyes lit up with delight. "Look at all this stuff!"

Against the wall were piles of old newspapers, perfect for making a new rat bed. In the corner was an old arm-chair with springs bursting out of its seat; it looked cozy enough for a rat family to move in straightaway. Over to the left were a few wooden tea crates full of old clothes, and beside them a large plastic shelving unit groaned under the weight of numerous tins and jars filled with pickles and fruit and vegetables and beans and meatballs. If Aldiss had known how to open them he would have had a rat feast right there and then. He licked his lips hungrily and rubbed his little hands together.

"This is brilliant!" he said in wonder. "A real treasure trove. I must remember where this house is so I can come back another time and help myself."

"You will not!" said Morag crossly. "That's stealing."

The rat looked round at her and frowned.

"Why do you care?" he asked. "You're running away."

"Well, I," she began, but she didn't really know how to answer. Aldiss had made a good point, so Morag said no more about it.

"Anyway, where's this tunnel?" she asked after a bit.

Bertie looked around. He seemed lost.

"I'm not sure," he said. "It was dark when we came up. Aldiss, have a sniff around and see if you can find the tunnel, will you? You might be bad at reading maps, but your nose has never let us down yet with finding tunnels."

"No problem," said Aldiss, taking a deep, enthusiastic sniff of the air. "I'll find it in no time."

As he scurried off, Morag had a look around. She stumbled across a pile of old clothes on the floor. Still cold, she sifted through them until she found an old woollen cardigan, which, although about three sizes too big for her, she put on under her housecoat. There was a pair of thick climber's socks and she slipped those on over her numb feet and then, best of all, she uncovered a pair of old green Wellington boots under a broken umbrella. They fit perfectly. For the first time in as long as she could remember, Morag felt quite pleased with herself. She might have looked a bit strange in her raggle-taggle clothes, and not at all trendy, but at least she was warm.

Bang! A door slammed in the kitchen above them. Morag, Bertie and Aldiss started and looked at each other.

"What was that?" whispered Bertie, his eyes wide with fright.

"It sounded like the back door," said Morag, who knew every sound in the house. Her stomach started doing backflips as she realized what was happening. "Oh no! Jermy and Moira must be coming back!"

"You don't think they'll come down here, do you?" asked a slightly hysterical Aldiss, who was usually scared of humans.

"I don't know," she replied. "But I'd hurry if I were you." Fearfully, she looked up at the cellar door, and for the first time, willed it not to open.

"Right," said Bertie, "let's find that tunnel."

Creak, creak, creak. The floorboards moved above them as Moira and Jermy walked into the kitchen. Morag crept up the cellar stairs to listen at the landing door. She could hear the low murmur of them talking and could just make out what they were saying.

"Don't you think it's time we let her out?" Jermy was asking. "She's been down there all day. And I'm starving."

"Just look at the mess she's made of our kitchen!" Moira whined. "She can clean it all up when we let her out, before she starts on our dinner. After that we might consider throwing her some leftovers—before we lock her back down there again!"

"Harsh but fair, Moira, my darling," said Jermy.

Listening to the two of them talk like that from behind the door made Morag feel sick.

"Come on, Jermy, my dear," Moira was cooing, "your program's on the telly. We'll let that little runt out in a while. We don't want her to think we're being too easy on her."

"Good idea, my love."

Morag sighed with relief as she heard their footsteps move out of the kitchen in the direction of the living room. As quietly as she could, she tiptoed down the stairs.

Bertie was sitting on the old burst armchair preening his feathers and Aldiss was having a good old root around in the piles of rubbish. All Morag could see were little flashes of brown fur and flicks of his long tail as he dived in and out of the great mounds of junk. All of a sudden there was a shout.

"Aha!" Aldiss emerged from a heap of old clothes. "I told you it was here!"

"You've found the tunnel?" Bertie asked excitedly and looked over at the little rat with great interest and hope.

"No," said Aldiss as he held up a moldy something in his paw. "But I have found that cheese I was telling you about."

31

Bertie's beady eyes narrowed. If looks could kill, then the look he gave Aldiss right then would have zapped the little rodent into oblivion.

"Just get on with finding the tunnel," said Bertie dryly, and with a salute the rat disappeared again. Sighing loudly, he motioned Morag over. "He may be some time. Come and sit with me here."

"So tell me about the mission you're going on," she asked, plonking herself down on the arm of the chair.

"Oh, I can't tell you about that! It's top secret," he replied, tapping the side of his large dark beak with a wing, as you would to tell people to mind their own business.

"Oh," said Morag with disappointment. Then she put her hand over her heart and, with a sincere look on her face, said, "I won't tell anyone, honestly. And even if I did, no one would believe me. I promise not to say a word."

He looked at her as if he were sizing her up. He hemmed and hawed for a few moments before talking again.

"Well," he began, "I suppose while we're waiting I could tell you a little bit. But then again, maybe I should say nothing. I'll have to think about it." He scrunched his face up as if thinking very hard. "Actually, I can't think of any reason why I shouldn't tell you. You seem like a trustworthy sort to me."

Morag leaned forward to hear better, her whole attention on the dodo. She loved a good story and had a feeling this was going to be one.

"So? What is it then?" she urged excitedly.

"Well . . . ," Bertie began.

Just then they were interrupted by a sharp noise from the top of the stairs. It sounded like scraping. It *was* something scraping. Someone was turning the key in the lock! Morag stared up at the door in horror and turned to Bertie.

"Oh no!" she said in a loud whisper. "They're coming! What are we going to do?" She felt sick. Jermy and Moira mustn't find her new friends; they would probably try and capture them and sell them online or to a circus.

"Oh, Aldiss, find the tunnel quickly!" she whispered. "Jermy and Moira are trying to open the door!"

"Yes, hurry," said Bertie. "We mustn't be found in here!"

The little rat heard the fear in their voices and scampered under the furniture. He searched beneath piles of old newspapers; he even sniffed behind an old desk in the corner, but found no trace of the tunnel.

"Hurry! Hurry!" Morag hissed. "They're trying different keys. They're coming!" She glanced up at the light coming from under the door. Whoever was trying to unlock it was having trouble, which was good for Aldiss because it gave him a little bit more time to find a way out. Rattle, rattle, rattle went the door handle. Then, click! The key turned in the lock and the door slowly squealed open. Morag's heart almost stopped with fright. And then . . .

"Here it is!" Aldiss called at last. "I've found it!" Bertie half flapped, half ran over to the little rat, who was jumping up and down with excitement. "It's this way," he said, pointing his little rat paw.

"Come on, Morag." Bertie waved at her to follow, but she hesitated. She knew she had to slow down Jermy and Moira.

"Hold on," she whispered. "I'll be there in a minute!"

She quickly got to her feet and leapt to the light switch. With a click, she flicked it off and the cellar was once again plunged into inky darkness.

"Damn!" said a startled voice from above. It was Moira. "The bulb must have blown." She called behind her, "Jermy, be a love and get me a new bulb."

"Do I have to do *everything*?" he whined. "Just tell her to come up the stairs and she can do it!"

There was a pause. "Good idea," said Moira. "Never thought of that."

"That's because you're thick as mince sometimes," said Jermy quietly.

"Oh! Is that so?" squealed Moira in a hurt voice. "You don't mean that, do you?"

"Just get the girl up here before I starve to death."

Down in the darkness, Morag crept carefully in the direction of Bertie and Aldiss. Ow! She stubbed her toe on the old burst armchair. Ouch! Tinkle. She elbowed over a glass jar. Oh! She tripped on the large pile of newspapers and they toppled with a whump to the floor.

"Morag! What are you doing down there?" Moira shouted crossly. "I hope you're not breaking anything, for if you are, you'll have me to answer to!"

But Morag didn't answer. She crouched and peered into the darkness. "Where are you?" she called softly. "Talk to me so I can hear you and work out which way to go."

"We're over here!" Bertie whispered back.

"Where?"

"Here!"

"Ow!" Her knee scraped on something sharp and she felt a sting. There was no time to check it, though. Jermy and Moira were about to come down. Ignoring the pain in her knee and the feeling of warm blood trickling down her shin, Morag picked herself up and continued crawling blindly in the direction of Bertie's voice.

"Morag? What are you doing down there? Come up here at once! Me and Jermy need our dinner!" shouted Moira angrily. "Do you hear me, girl? Morag! MORAG! She's not answering me, Jermy," she said crossly.

"Bertie? Aldiss? Are you still there?" Morag whispered.

"Yes," answered Bertie. "You're nearly here, another few steps and . . . Oops, careful of that old tea set. There you are!"

She stretched out her hands and felt the soft springy feathers of her new friend. She grinned to herself in the dark.

"I can't see a thing," she confessed.

"Don't worry, we're at the tunnel. Keep ahold of me and I'll guide you through."

Carefully and quietly she edged along until she felt the rim of a hole with her foot.

"Is this it?" she asked anxiously.

"Yes," whispered Bertie from inside. "Sit yourself down and let yourself drop. Come on—we don't have much time. I think your friends will be on us any second now!"

"They're not my friends," said Morag.

"Moira!" Jermy's voice echoed down into the cellar. "Haven't you got ahold of that brat yet?"

"She's hiding from me," answered Moira. "I've shouted and shouted, but she won't respond. You don't think she's dead, do you?"

"Dead? She'll wish she was when I get ahold of her."

Morag heard the familiar heavy thunder of Jermy's footsteps stalk toward the door at the top of the landing. There was a pause while, she supposed, he was working out what to do next, and then she heard him creep slowly down the stairs. Blink! The light went on. Morag screwed up her eyes in the sudden glare, and from her position on the floor she could see Jermy's legs through the jumble of chairs, up-turned tables and sagging boxes. He was looking around for her. As quietly as she could, she pushed herself further into the hole. It was only big enough for her to squeeze in and no more. She ducked down inside just as Jermy spotted her.

"Hoi! What do you think you're doing?" he demanded, as he leapt toward her, his arm outstretched.

But Morag was gone.

Slipping and sliding down the tunnel for what seemed like an age, she eventually came out with a plop into something like a small cave. Thud! Her bottom hit the soft earth and moss below and there she stayed until she was able to catch her breath.

"Bertie? Aldiss?" she whispered in the semidarkness. "Are you still there?"

From nowhere a little blue light bobbed toward her and stopped. Before her, Bertie's hooked beak emerged. In his right wing he held a large blue stone that glowed softly. Morag stared at it; it was beautiful.

"Are you all right?" the dodo asked kindly. "You're not injured or anything?" Morag shook her head. "Good," he said. "Now follow me. We don't have much time." He saw Morag looking at the stone. "A Moonstone," he explained, holding it up. "Great for lighting up tunnels. Now, we must hurry. We've wasted enough time already."

"But where are we going?" asked Morag, scrambling to her hands and knees. She couldn't stand up, as the tunnel was too small. Down a dusty, narrow passageway she crawled after Bertie.

"To release Shona," he replied over his shoulder. "She's been a prisoner, like you, for too long."

"Shona? Who's Shona?" asked Morag. "And where is she being held prisoner?"

In the gloom, she could make out a little smile playing around the edges of Bertie's beak.

"You'll see," he said, and he hurried her further down the tunnel until the barking echoes of Moira and Jermy became faint, and then they could hear them no more.

4

Deep under the earth, the tunnel wound for what seemed like miles, on and on, up and down, round and round until Morag was quite dizzy and her knees started to hurt. Down there, it was dark and dusty and the air was slightly stale. The tunnels weren't made for Big People, Bertie told her as they hurried further into the darkness, they were made by the little people so they could go about their business without the Big People—humans—trying to catch them and put them in cages. There were thousands of underground tunnels, Bertie revealed, and they went everywhere.

"So where are the little people now?" Morag asked, full of curiosity. She looked around, trying to imagine lots of little men and women running up and down the small tunnels. "Are they still here? Do they still use the tunnels?"

"Not so much," said Bertie, adjusting his little satchel that was casually slung across his shoulders. "They only use them when they absolutely have to. They don't often leave to go anywhere—it's too dangerous for them now."

"Leave? Leave where?" Morag was intrigued. Was there a special place where little people lived?

"Marnoch—," began Aldiss excitedly.

"Aldiss!" snapped Bertie. "That's enough. We mustn't tell her any more. It just wouldn't do."

It wasn't only Aldiss who jumped at Bertie's harsh tone. Morag too was taken aback. She looked at the bird, startled that he had spoken in such a way.

"Why won't you tell me anything?" she asked. "Don't you think I can be trusted?" She felt a little bit hurt by this. She was the most trustworthy person she knew. She could keep a secret and had never betrayed anyone's trust, ever.

Bertie stopped in his tracks and turned to face Morag.

"Miss Morag," he began, his face serious. "It's not that we don't trust you," he said. "But we've only just met you and after all, you're one of them. A Big Person. And our experience of Big People is that they cannot be trusted. Not ever, not anyhow, not anywhere. It's nothing personal, it's just . . ."

"That you won't trust me," finished Morag, her voice full of dejection.

Bertie looked a little embarrassed. "Well, yes," he said. "But you must understand, it's not because of who you are, it's because of what you are . . . a human. We don't know you well enough to tell you anything. After all, how do we know you won't go and spill our secrets to the world? How do we know you won't tell everything to other Big People and then they'll come and try and track down Marn . . . I mean, our living place, and then there would be nothing left? Do you understand me? I'm trying to protect folk like me and Aldiss."

Morag nodded. "I understand," she said a little glumly, for she was desperate to know Bertie's secrets and she was upset that he wouldn't tell her, but she understood. If he were to tell, it could put others in danger. "I'm sorry for asking," she said.

"I'm sorry I can't tell you anything," replied Bertie sorrowfully. "You seem like a nice girl, but we'll be leaving you soon to go on with our mission and you'll do whatever it is you humans do."

Morag didn't reply to this. She merely smiled a little bit, although she really didn't feel like smiling at all considering she didn't know what she was going to do once they'd got out of the tunnel. However, giving Bertie a little smile seemed like the best thing to do. Where she was going to go and what she was going to do with herself weighed heavily on her mind. One thing she did know was that she was never, ever going back to live with Jermy and Moira. She couldn't now.

"Here we are!" Aldiss's high-pitched voice broke into her thoughts. They had reached an area where, Morag saw, the tunnel started to widen. As they continued, it got broader and taller until she was able to stand up without slouching. She was relieved, as her legs and arms were aching from all the crawling and she was covered from head to toe in dust.

The girl, the rat and the dodo came out into a small chamber illuminated by clusters of Moonstones set into the rocks at regular intervals above their heads. The stones served as lamps and made the little cave seem quite bright. A little further away, Morag could make out a faint tinge of real moonlight falling through a hole in the cave wall, and already she could smell the sea air and hear the crash of the waves somewhere below them. She guessed they must be somewhere in the hills overlooking the beach.

Bertie sighed, ruffled his feathers and turned to Morag.

"Well, my dear," he said, "I suppose it's time we said good-bye to you and went our separate ways. Aldiss and I have a very big job to do and we must press on. It was very nice to meet you." He held out a wing for her to shake.

"And you too," she said, shaking his wing. And he turned away and started to walk toward the cave's exit.

"Good-bye, Morag," said Aldiss a little regretfully, and he gave her a salute. "It's been a pleasure to know you."

"Good-bye." She sighed and suddenly felt very lonely. "And good luck with your mission," she called as the dodo and the rat made for the exit of the cave. She sighed again, and tears began to prick her eyes. She stifled a sob. "Good luck," she whispered sadly, and sat down on the floor of the cave. She watched as the dodo waddled and the little rat scampered out of view behind the rocks. Then she pulled her knees up to her chest, buried her head in her arms and burst into tears. She could hardly contain the great big sobs that seemed to start from her stomach and erupt through her chest. Hot, salty tears ran down her face as she cried her little heart out. She had no one to love and no one loved her, she realized. There was nowhere to go, and she was completely and utterly alone. This made her cry all the more.

Something touched her shoulder gently. She looked up and saw the furry little face of Aldiss looking at her intently. His beady black eyes were welling up with tears of sympathy.

"Are you all right?" he asked. "What's the matter?"

"Oh, hello again," said Morag, suddenly very embarrassed, as she hadn't expected anyone to find her crying. She wiped her eyes and sniffed. "I'm okay, honestly," she assured him. "I'm just . . . I'm just . . ." But she could find no explanation as to why she was crying other than the truth. "I'm just sad." She sobbed. "Because I have nowhere to go. I have no one to go to."

"Oh dear," replied the rat. "That's terrible. No one at all?" He patted her hand kindly. Morag shook her head.

"Then you must come with us!" he squeaked, his little black eyes lit up with excitement.

"I couldn't do that," began Morag uncertainly. "Could I?"

"Of course you could," replied the rodent with a whiskery smile. "It makes perfect sense."

"But what about Bertie?" asked Morag, beginning to feel a bit better. "He won't want me. Won't he be angry you've asked me?"

"You leave him to me!" Aldiss said decisively.

"Leave who to whom?" It was Bertie. Morag and Aldiss looked round to see the fat dodo standing in the mouth of the cave, looking a little cross. "Aldiss, I've been searching for you everywhere. I thought you had fallen off the dunes and into the sea. I really did. I spent ages peering over the edge looking for you. What are you doing back here anyway?"

"Well," said Aldiss, looking down at the ground and shifting dust with one of his paws. "I just came back because I wanted to see that Morag was all right. And she wasn't. Oh, Bertie, she has nowhere to go and no one to go to. It's so sad. So I said she could come with us. That's okay, isn't it?"

"Oh, for goodness' sake!" exclaimed Bertie crossly. He hit his brow with a wing in frustration. "How many times do I have to tell you not to pick up waifs and strays? Eh? How many times? But you will insist on doing it. Remember that bear you wanted to keep as a pet?" he huffed.

"But I loved Snowy," insisted Aldiss. "He just didn't love me."

"He tried to eat you!" said Bertie.

"That wasn't his fault," retorted the rat.

Bertie huffed again. He paused before he began to speak. "Look, I've told you before, Morag cannot come with us. It's too dangerous."

"Please let me come," said Morag. "I'll be a great help, really I will, and Aldiss did say having a Big Person would come in useful. Didn't you, Aldiss?" The rat nodded enthusiastically in agreement.

The dodo looked at Morag, whose eyes were brimming with tears again. He looked at Aldiss. The rat wasn't actually crying, but he was dabbing his eyes with a paw.

"Please, Bertie," pleaded Aldiss. "She won't be any trouble, will you, Morag?"

Morag shook her head.

Bertie sighed the resigned sigh of someone who knew he was well and truly defeated. He knew he shouldn't trust a human, but there was something about Morag he couldn't help liking. He decided to take a chance on her.

"Very well," he said. Morag squealed and clapped her hands in delight. "But you must do everything I tell you, is that understood?"

"Absolutely!" said Morag. "Anything you say."

"Now, you two," he said curtly. "Enough of this idle chitchat, we have work to do. Shona cannot free herself."

Morag got to her feet. "Of course, I forgot," she said. "Shona. Who is she and why is she in prison?"

"Prison? I never said she was in prison," replied Bertie a little grumpily. He still wasn't sure that bringing a human child along was such a good idea, especially now she had started asking difficult questions.

"But you said she was a prisoner and you and Aldiss had to free her." Morag was confused. As she followed the dodo and the rat to the mouth of the cave, she felt fresh sea air blow in from outside. After being stuck in the stuffiness of the dusty tunnel for ages, the crisp, cold, salt-scented air felt like a godsend. She inhaled deeply.

"Yes I did," said Bertie. "But poor dear Shona is not in a prison as you'd understand it. No, she has suffered a much worse fate than that."

"What do you mean?" Morag asked. It was dark

outside and the storm was starting to move off. Rain was still falling, but not as harshly as before, and the wind, though still chilly, had died down a good bit. She pulled her housecoat and cardigan around her all the tighter.

"I take it you know Irvine Beach well?" said Bertie.

"Yes, I've lived here all my life," she replied. "Why? Is Shona being kept a prisoner near here?" She was puzzled. She didn't know of any prisons in the area nor did she know of any houses or buildings where Shona might be kept, except perhaps the abandoned lighthouse at the end of the beach.

"You could say that," said Bertie smugly. "On top of the hills overlooking the sea there's a large brick dragon. Have you seen it?"

"Yes. I used to play up there," replied Morag. She frowned. "I loved climbing on it. I would pretend it could fly. It would take me out to sea and far away from here. Why do you mention it?"

Bertie opened his beak to speak, but his rat friend got in ahead of him.

"That dragon *is* Shona!" exclaimed an excited Aldiss triumphantly. Then he saw Bertie's angry face and shied away. "Sorry, Bertie, I couldn't hold it in any longer."

"Quite," said Bertie curtly. "The dragon is indeed Shona. She's not really made of brick. She was a living dragon once. She could talk and walk. I'm not sure if she could fly. They say she was a beautiful creature, quite lovely. Big yellow eyes and a deep emerald-colored hide. She was very striking. And a great conversationalist.

Terrific sense of humor. Everyone was devastated when Devlish took her and made her into what she is now."

"Devlish? Who's he?" Morag wanted to know.

Aldiss looked about himself fearfully. "An evil male witch, a warlock," he said. "He's a dreadful being. Truly evil. You don't want to mess with him."

"But I don't understand. Why did he turn Shona into a pile of bricks?"

"Well . . . ," Bertie began.

"She wouldn't do what he wanted," interrupted Aldiss. "She wouldn't carry out his evil plans, so he bewitched her into stone."

"Aldiss!" said Bertie crossly. He stamped a claw and flapped his little wings in frustration. "Can't I tell a story from start to finish? Must you always interrupt?"

"Sorry, Bertie." The little rodent hung his head and shuffled off to the side as if trying to disappear.

"I'm sure he didn't mean to interrupt, did you, Aldiss?" Morag said kindly. Aldiss shook his head. "Bertie, why don't you finish the story? How long has she been like that?"

"Oh, for decades now," the dodo replied sadly. "And they say she was once an amazing creature."

"Why didn't anyone free her before?"

"We tried, but we couldn't. Devlish's magic was too strong. Look, why don't we sit down and wait until this rain goes off and I'll tell you all about it? I think we've got a good half an hour before this storm passes over us."

So the three friends each found a rock to sit on at the

cave mouth and looked out at the dark, rain-lashed waves. And while they waited, Bertie related a tale to Morag that was so amazing it made her mouth fall open and her eyes widen in surprise.

What he told her was this: he and Aldiss came from the secret northern kingdom of Marnoch Mor, high up in the Highlands. Hidden in the mountains and protected by magic, Marnoch Mor is home to the magic folk—fairies and kelpies, gnomes and wizards, witches and elves. It is also home to many mythical creatures, including griffins and unicorns. And then there are the animals, including those that man thought extinct, such as dodos.

"Many years ago, when the moon and the sun were younger," said Bertie, "the mythical creatures and the animals shared the earth. They lived with mankind in harmony until an evil male witch, the warlock Devlish, rose up out of their tribes. He told men that the powers of the magic folk could be used to their advantage and turned mankind against them. Battles ensued. Most of the royal family were murdered and those of the magic folk who weren't enslaved had to go into hiding. They fled to the hills and called their settlement Marnoch Mor, and to protect them from being found by the outside world they used the magical power of the Eye of Lornish.

"It's a really beautiful place," Bertie continued, smiling. "There are towering waterfalls and serene lochs and impossible mountains and fields full of fruit that haven't been seen in this world since the magic folk left it. Our ancestors all worked together to make Marnoch Mor a lovely place, and everyone lived in peace, and the present inhabitants strive to keep it that way. Now, before you say anything, Aldiss, I admit it: we sometimes have the odd argument, but nothing serious. With the Eye of Lornish to protect us, we normally have nothing to fear from the outside world. . . . There was no chance of us being discovered, you see.

"Then something terrible happened." Bertie's little black eyes were full of fear. "Not long ago, Devlish—"

"He's still alive after all this time?" interrupted an astonished Morag.

Aldiss shook his head. "No, it's his great-great-great-great-great-great-great-great grandson, Devlish the Tenth."

"Anyway," the dodo resumed. "Devlish—the Tenth—has stolen the Eye of Lornish and left us unprotected. Now the outside world is breaking in and Marnoch Mor is crumbling. If we don't do something now, it will cease to exist altogether. After that, who knows what Devlish will do with the Eye? We fear that he may try to use it to conquer this world and that would be disastrous. He's already enslaved some humans and animals to do his spying and evil work for him. If he is allowed to carry on, who knows what he'll do?"

"But can't someone stop him?" cried Morag. "Don't you have a witch or wizard or warlock strong enough to fight him?"

"The great Highland wizard, Montgomery, has already challenged Devlish on the theft of the Eye and demanded its return. Devlish denies all knowledge of the theft and claims he is being victimized by Montgomery and the rest of the WWWC."

"The WWWC? What's that?" asked Morag. Her head was beginning to hurt with all this new information. She was still finding it hard to accept that talking animals, let alone witches and wizards, actually existed.

"The Witches', Warlocks' and Wizards' Convention," explained Bertie. "It is they who govern Marnoch Mor and make sure no bad ever befalls the kingdom. Montgomery is this year's chairman of the WWWC and, naturally, our Queen Flora is the head of the Convention."

"And the Eye of . . . what was it called?"

"Lornish. The Eye of Lornish," said Aldiss. "It's a magical stone from the bottom of the Seas of Lornish. It fell from the sky when the world was being made, or so our ancestors told us. It's been smoothed over thousands of years by the currents and the sands of the sea. It sparkles like the stars it left behind. It's very powerful and is imbued with ancient magic."

"Seas of Lornish?" queried Morag, who had never heard of them.

"You would know it as the North Sea," Bertie said quickly, before Aldiss could.

"I see," said Morag. "And where does Shona fit in to all of this?"

"Shona," began Bertie, "is the only good-hearted creature left alive who knows how to get to the Island of Murst . . . that's where Devlish lives."

"Where in the world is that?"

"The Island of Murst," he went on, "is thought to be located somewhere near the Western Isles, off the west coast of Scotland. No human map shows the island because, to all intents and purposes, it doesn't exist in the human world.

"Now, to find it, one must use magic," Bertie continued. "Montgomery and his fellow WWWC members have tried and failed to locate it with their powers, but Shona was hatched on the island. It was home to an empire of dragons like her, but Devlish had his henchmen hunt them down and interrogate them about the Early Secrets of Murst. None of them would talk and he killed them off one by one until only she survived. And then, once he realized she was loyal to the memory of her race and wouldn't cooperate, he turned her into a pile of bricks to be a living memorial to them. Apart from Devlish's own people, Shona is the only creature who knows how to get there."

"That's awful," said Morag, her eyes wide with amazement. "So, are we going to free her and then go to Murst and get the Eye?"

"Well, not quite," said Bertie. "Montgomery has given us the task of freeing Shona. He knows how to do it now, you see. He finally uncovered the spell in an ancient book in the Great Library at Marnoch Mor, the one that's in the Museum of Weird Things and Magic. He chose me to carry the task out because"—and here he paused for effect— "well, I don't want to blow my own trumpet, but he chose me because I'm the best pupil in his magic school. He whispered the secret spell with which I will unlock the enchantment that keeps Shona a stone dragon. I am so honored; it's such a great thing to be doing this for so great a man. I can't believe he chose me, though of course my grades are always the best in the class and—"

"Ahem!" Aldiss interrupted, and Bertie pulled himself together.

"Oh yes," the dodo said, suddenly remembering he was relating a story. "I have to free her and then send for Montgomery, who will go to Murst and retrieve the Eye of Lornish."

"Hmm," said Morag as she looked up at the sky. The rain was going off and the sky didn't look quite as murderous as it had earlier. "If Montgomery is so great, why didn't he come here and free Shona himself? Surely that would have been a better plan?"

"Er, yes, maybe, if the WWWC's AGM hadn't been taking place."

"AGM?"

"Annual General Meeting," he explained. "Montgomery has to be there to chair the meeting. If he's not, Devlish will know something is going on and will try to stop it. Our best weapon against him is surprise. If we can get Shona free without him finding out, Montgomery has a better chance of getting to Murst undetected. It's a quite brilliant plan," the dodo added triumphantly.

"The rain's off!" squeaked Aldiss excitedly. Bertie and Morag looked outside. Sure enough, the dark evening sky—now bright with the white light of the full moon— was clear of any rain clouds.

"Well, Miss Morag," said Bertie, turning and looking

51

her straight in the eye. "This could be very dangerous. For one thing, we don't know what kind of mood Shona will be in when we free her. Dragons are notoriously bad tempered. She might attack us! Are you sure you don't want to go home?"

Morag had a great big beaming smile on her face. "And miss out on meeting a real live dragon?" she said breathlessly. "I most definitely still want to come. I've never been on an adventure before."

"We'd best be off, then," replied the dodo. "We've no time to lose."

5

First Bertie, then Aldiss, then Morag scuttled out of the safety of the cave and along a narrow path that followed the winding escarpment of the hilltop and eventually joined the sand dunes on the edge of the beach. The dune grasses brushed gently against her pajama trousers as Morag tried to keep up with the fast pace of her two new friends. Before they had left the cave, Bertie had warned her that Devlish's spies were everywhere and that she should keep an eye out for any animal or human that looked dangerous. She followed them uneasily, her eyes darting from side to side, trying to see beyond the dark outcrops of grasses.

"How will I know them?" she asked nervously.

"Oh, you'll know them all right," replied Aldiss

fearfully. He leant over and whispered to her: "Their eyes glow in the dark!"

So there they were, a girl in a housecoat, a rat and a dodo, running unsteadily along the soft sandy path. Morag stumbled a few times in the dry sand and fell to her knees once, but she got back to her feet quickly and hurried after Bertie and Aldiss. Although it was still very cold, she did not have time to feel the chill. Running along the dunes left her hot, sweaty and breathless. The blustery sea air whipped sand in her eyes, but she kept going, grateful that at least it had stopped raining. She would have felt quite miserable running in the rain. After what seemed like an age, Bertie came to a sudden stop and held up his wing. Panting, Aldiss stopped, with Morag behind him.

"We're here," said Bertie. "Look!"

Against the darkness of the moonlit sky, Morag could just make out the small hilltop on which curled the great brick body of the dragon on Irvine Beach, except the poor soul had a name now: Shona. She looked so sad and forlorn sitting up there, staring out to sea, that Morag felt tears of pity well up in her eyes. She blinked them back quickly.

"Shona," whispered Morag, slightly awestruck. She was a little breathless from the running, but it didn't stop her from being impressed by being in the company of a real, and almost living, dragon.

"Yes," said Bertie. "*That* is Shona."

They all stood in silence for a moment, gazing up at the bulky shape of the dragon edged in moonlight and silhouetted against the dark winter sky. Bertie gave the signal for the off again and they all ran up the hill to the edge of the mound on which Shona sat. Morag had never really thought much about the dragon before and felt almost ashamed that she had often used Shona as a plaything, clambering all over her body and sitting on her tail, little realizing that she had once been a living creature. The dragon took on a whole new meaning for her, and she ran up to her and looked into her large blank stone eyes, searching for a glimmer of life. The dragon continued to stare past her, out to sea, her eyes as dead as the brick they were made from. Morag gently stroked her cold hard muzzle and hoped that deep down Shona somehow knew Morag was there for her.

"She's not very big for a dragon, is she?" said Morag, who thought all dragons were huge, ferocious beasts. "I'm sure elephants are bigger."

"Not all dragons are big," replied Bertie knowingly. He took his satchel from his shoulders and opened it. He pulled out a Moonstone and gave it to Aldiss. "Hold it over my bag, please, so I can see what I'm doing," he instructed, and the rat did as he was bid. As the stone lit up the two animals and Shona, Bertie continued to talk. "No," he said, rummaging about in the bag. "Shona's a pygmy dragon. You only get them on Murst, or rather . . . you only *got* them on Murst. She's the last of her kind. Ah, here it is!"

He pulled out a small leather pouch and opened it. Dipping his beak inside he took out, one by one, six large white stones with strange markings on them. "Runes," he told Morag, and placed them carefully on his wing tip.

"Now, I will ask for silence, please," he said authoritatively.

"What are you going to do with them?" asked Morag, breaking the silence as her curiosity got the better of her.

"Shhhh!" said Bertie. "I *will* have quiet while I perform the ritual!" But his instructions fell on deaf ears, as Morag was so excited about the prospect of seeing authentic magic in action that she could not help speaking.

"What's he going to do with those?" she whispered to Aldiss.

The rat shrugged before answering matter-of-factly: "Just a ritual."

Bertie shushed them both again. This time Morag stayed quiet and watched with interest. The dodo closed his eyes and took a deep breath.

"Om-a-loma-loma-lummmmmmmm!" he cried as he raised the runes up over his head. They shook a little against his feathers. "Oooooma-loooma-loooma-looooo!" he went on. The runes began to shake even more. "Arno, jarno, sharno, kaaaaa!" And with a loud squawk and a flourish, Bertie threw the runes to the hard sandy ground at Shona's tail.

"What's happening?" Morag whispered to Aldiss.

"He's just thrown the rune stones onto the sand," he whispered carefully, as if he were describing something Morag didn't already know.

"I can see that," she whispered a little grumpily. "But *why?*"

"Don't know," replied the rat. "Don't do magic myself."

"Right," said Morag. This rat was exasperating at times. She decided not to ask any more questions and just watched. Bertie held a wing tip up to his beak as he studied the stones lying higgledy-piggledy on the sand beneath his claws. His brow furrowed into a deep frown, and he said "hmm" a lot.

"I see," he said after a bit. "It's all come quite right now. I know what to do."

"What? What do they say?" asked Morag animatedly. She'd never seen anyone use rune stones before and couldn't help being excited. "Can I help? Can I do something?"

Bertie gave her an imperious look, as if someone had done something nasty to produce a bad smell, and shook his head.

"Thank you, but no thank you," he said haughtily. "Only those who understand magic can do this. Now, can I ask you and Aldiss to stand back down the hill while I try to bring Shona back to life? This could be dangerous."

Disappointed, Morag didn't say anything else and followed Aldiss down the hill a bit. The rat found a comfortable tuft of grass to sit on and offered her a space next to him. She sat down and watched as Bertie, illuminated by the Moonstone, prepared the spell. He picked up the runes and placed them very carefully at intervals along the dragon's back. He then went to the tip of its nose and bowed very low. He closed his eyes again. Then he began to chant in a language unfamiliar to Morag.

"Orimar, animar, ento larn," he sang. "Metreon, activer, neo, garf!" Or at least, that was what the words sounded like to Morag. He continued to chant, and as he did, something strange began to happen. The wind that had been blowing the grasses around them suddenly dropped, and there was no sound at all except for Bertie's chanting.

Startled by the sudden quiet, Morag looked around. She could still just about make out the waves lapping against the shore below, but she couldn't hear them as clearly as before. She could see the wind wafting through the grasses on the dunes nearby, but there was no wind where she was. She knew she was at the beach, but she could no longer smell the saltiness of the air, nor taste the grit of sand in her mouth. It was as if they were all being held inside an invisible bubble of something magical.

Suddenly the dragon's body lit up a bright and vivid green, and white sparks flew from its head and tail. Morag watched fascinated as, with a whizzing noise, the sparks grew bigger and changed color from white to green, to red to purple, to blue to yellow, and then to orange. And still Bertie continued to chant.

Then something marvelous happened: the dragon's body began to change from red brick to flesh. Gone were the rough, chunky shapes of the red bricks, replaced by smooth, shiny green scales. Morag saw the black claws appear on Shona's feet, and then the armored point of her tail became visible. Moments later the ears, the eyes, the jaw and the teeth could be seen. Bertie's voice began to get louder and then rose to a shout.

"Becknar Dort!" he called. "Shona! Great dragon of Murst! I command you to open your eyes!"

Morag held her breath and heard Aldiss gasp.

Nothing happened.

Bertie tried again.

"Shona! Great dragon of Murst! I command you . . . !"

"All right, all right, I heard you the first time," came a low grumbling voice. "Although I think you might have asked more politely." The dragon opened her startlingly yellow eyes and looked down at the dodo. "Oh!" she said. "I thought it might have been a more impressive wizard who finally freed me."

"Albert Alonzo Fluke at your service, madam," said Bertie, bowing very low. "But you may call me Bertie."

The dragon looked a little bemused. She yawned and showed off a set of ferocious yellow teeth and a long curling tongue. Bertie stepped back a little nervously as the jaws closed back together. The dragon stretched her neck and rolled her shoulders. She closed her eyes and enjoyed the freedom of moving. Then she stretched her front legs, her spine and her hind legs and tail. Finally, she stood up unsteadily.

"Oooh, I've been dying to do that for thirty years," she said. Having been in the same position for decades, her legs were not used to carrying her and she had to sit back down again with a bump.

"Perhaps you should rest for a bit," suggested Morag.

The dragon turned her catlike eyes on the girl. She looked at her intently, hungrily, as if she were sizing Morag up as a possible next meal.

"*What*, might I ask, are *you*?" Shona asked sleepily. She yawned again.

"A girl. Morag," said Morag, scrambling to her feet to give the dragon a little curtsy. "And this," she said, indicating the trembling rat, "is my friend Aldiss Drinkwater."

"Hi!" squeaked the rat.

The dragon's eyes swiveled to where Morag had pointed. She looked hard and frowned.

"*What* is Aldiss Drinkwater?" she asked. "I can't see anything in this light. My eyes aren't what they used to be. Where is Aldiss Drinkwater? Stand forward, man, so I can see you."

Aldiss leapt off the clump of dune grass and scrambled up the hill. He stopped halfway between Morag and the dragon and gave a smart salute. "Hello!" he called.

Shona frowned again and leant over for a better look. Then she caught sight of Aldiss.

"Oh! Oh!" she squealed, recoiling in horror. "A rat! Oh! A rat! Oh, I hate rats! They're dirty, horrible things! Get it away from me! Get it away!"

She staggered back from the startled rat and almost went over the hilltop. "Oh, get it away from me!" she begged Morag and Bertie. Morag was shocked. She hadn't expected this. She moved forward toward the dragon, who was now standing on the edge of the hill, shaking like Jell-O and whimpering quietly.

"It's all right, Shona," Morag said softly. "Aldiss won't hurt you. He's really very nice."

"How do you *know*?" Shona cried. "How do you *know*? He might look cute, but he's not. None of them are. They wait until you're asleep and then bite you, that's what rats do. They nibble on your toes and eat your food and tear up your bedding and take over your lair. That's what rats do. My uncle Larrs wasn't the same after his cave was infested with them. Urgh! They're horrible, squeaking things with vile, hairless tails."

"Excuse me, Madam Dragon," Bertie interjected. "I can assure you that Aldiss is nothing of the kind. He's one of the most decent chaps I know. And additionally, we would never have got here to free you if it hadn't been for him," he announced, winking at the startled rat. "He's a champion map reader, you know!"

Shona didn't look convinced.

"*And* he's very caring," said Morag.

"*And* I've never nibbled on anyone's toes in my life," piped up Aldiss enthusiastically, although he was a bit peeved to be accused of such a thing.

"Ummm," said Shona, still unconvinced.

Aldiss stepped forward again, causing the dragon to curl up in fright.

"Madam Dragon," said Aldiss graciously. "Please will you come back from the edge and make friends with me. I promise I won't bite you or eat your food or infest your lair."

"Aldiss is a very nice rat who has been brought up properly by a very nice family. His mother would be horrified if she heard what you're saying about rats," said Bertie.

Shona looked from Bertie to Morag to Aldiss and back to Bertie.

"All right," she said uncertainly. She took an unsteady

step toward them. "But only if you can assure me he's perfectly safe."

"He is!" Morag and Bertie said together.

"I am!" said Aldiss.

"Okay," said the dragon. Gingerly she moved toward the top of the cliff and sat down again. She was quivering from the effort. She was still recovering from being enchanted for so long and was quite exhausted. Eventually she calmed down and was able to think about more pressing matters.

"What's for supper?" she asked after a bit.

"Ah, yes!" said Bertie quickly. He rummaged about in his satchel and produced a bottle of pickled onions. Morag scowled. There was something familiar about that jar—it had come from Jermy and Moira's basement! Shona's yellow eyes lit up and she licked her lips. Dragons love pickled onions. Bertie struggled to open the jar with his beak and went quite red in the face with effort. Morag took pity on him and whisked the jar off him and, with a quick twist, had the jar open and offered it to the dragon. Gently, Shona took the jar and tipped the entire contents down her throat in one go.

As she watched the dragon eat, Morag suddenly remembered how hungry she was herself, and her stomach rumbled. She looked at Bertie.

"Don't suppose you have anything else in there, do you?" she asked.

"What would you like?" he responded.

"What have you got?" said Morag.

"Anything you desire," he replied with a smile. Morag was confused. The satchel was quite small, so it couldn't possibly hold very much. She decided to be cheeky and ask for something Bertie couldn't possibly have in his satchel.

"I would like," she said, "a tall glass of hot chocolate and a plate of toasted marshmallows." Her eyes were on Bertie to see his reaction.

"No problem," he said and stuck a wing down into his satchel. He brought out a steaming hot chocolate, quickly followed by a plate of warmly toasted pink and white marshmallows. He handed them to an astonished Morag.

"How did you do *that*?" she asked, her mouth open in wonder. She suddenly had a new respect for Bertie.

"Well, it's not that easy," Bertie began.

"Yes it is!" interrupted Aldiss. Behind him, Shona jumped in fright. She was still scared of the rat, but he didn't seem to notice. "That's a magic satchel, that is!" he announced. "It will give you any kind of food or drink you want. Watch! Bertie, could you get me a large piece of chocolate cake and a small glass of milk, please?"

Bertie, who was a little bit annoyed by Aldiss's interruption *and* the fact that the rat had told everyone his secret, nevertheless placed his wing in the satchel and pulled out a deliciously moist piece of cake and a small glass of milk. He handed them to Aldiss, who wolfed them down. The milk left a white rim around the rat's little mouth and dripped from his whiskers as he smiled in satisfaction.

"That is a fantastic bag!" said Morag. "Can I have a go?" She reached over to take the satchel from Bertie, but before the dodo could voice an objection, they were disturbed by a rustling in the long grass on the sand dunes behind them. The magic bubble that had earlier surrounded them had by now melted away, and they could hear the sounds of the waves and the winds around them once more.

"What's that?" asked Aldiss, startled. His whiskers were quivering with fright. He sniffed long and deep. "Oh no!" His eyes widened in terror.

Bertie ran over to him. "What? What?" he said, alarmed.

Aldiss looked at his friend with real fear in his beady little black eyes. "I smell a . . . a . . . Klapp demon!" he squeaked, and ran behind Morag for safety. Bertie looked sick.

"What's a Klapp demon?" asked Morag, concerned now for the safety of her new friends and herself. She definitely *didn't* like the sound of this new creature.

"A Klapp demon—" began Bertie.

"Is trouble!" Shona finished. "You must find it and kill it," she said to the dodo. "Before it gets away!"

"Kill it?" said Morag, who hated the thought of killing anything. "But why?"

"Because it will tell," Bertie said simply, eyes darting about looking for the Klapp demon. He cocked his head to the side and listened. Then he began to run hither and thither about the hilltop, holding a Moonstone high above his head to give him as much light as it could.

"I don't understand. *Who* will it tell? *What* will it tell?" Morag asked.

"My dear Morag," Bertie answered, puffing slightly from the effort of his search. "If we don't find it and kill it, it will go back to Devlish and tell him what's been going on here and he will find us and turn us all into stone—or something much worse! We *cannot* let it escape. Now, come and help me find it before it's too late!"

Shona was still too weak to help with the hunt, so she rested on the hilltop while Morag, Bertie and Aldiss searched the surrounding sand dunes.

Morag had no clue as to what kind of creature she was supposed to be looking for, but continued the pursuit of the elusive Klapp demon along with the other two. After about half an hour of frantic searching, the trio finally gave up.

"It's no use," said Bertie anxiously. "It's gone. Oh dear, oh dear, oh dear. This is not good. Montgomery will be furious. He specifically instructed me to free Shona without alerting Devlish, and now I've let him down. What am I going to do?"

He plonked himself down on a tuft of dune grass and

put his head under his wing. Morag could hear little muffled sobs coming from under the feathers. She didn't understand why he was so upset.

"Maybe it's not so bad," she said as she sat down beside him. She put her arm around his shoulders and felt the dodo shuddering. "Maybe it wasn't a Klapp demon after all, and we have nothing to worry about."

"It *was* a Klapp demon all right," said Aldiss. "There's nothing smells as awful and as musty and as stinky as a Klapp demon."

"He's right," said Shona, who didn't appear to be as afraid of the rat anymore. "They are horrible things. Worse than ra . . . worse than a lot of things," she quickly corrected herself. She looked guiltily at Aldiss, who hadn't noticed she'd nearly said "rats."

Aldiss shuddered. "Yeuch," he said.

Morag looked at Shona.

"What are they, anyway? They can't be *that* bad, surely?" she said.

Shona made a face. "Oh yes they can," she said. "I remember them well. They are ugly apelike creatures with long arms and legs. They have straggly, matted fur, big googly eyes and sharp teeth to tear away the flesh of the dead things they eat, and the more rotten the better. They have the worst breath on earth and large ears to listen in on people, so that they can tell Devlish what they've heard. They don't care about anything other than gold, and Devlish gives them plenty of that to do his dirty work for him."

"Are there lots of Klapp demons?" asked Morag.

"There's a family of about sixty of them called the Meermores, headed up by the Grand Pappy Meermore. There were more Klapp demon families, but the Meermores killed and ate them. They are downright wicked, creeping about everywhere, spying on innocent folk." Shona made a disgusted face when she said this.

"Then why have I never seen one?" Morag said, for she was sure she would have remembered them.

"Oh, they're very good at hiding," said Aldiss.

"Haven't you ever thought you've caught sight of something out of the side of your eye," said Shona, "and turned only to see that whatever it was had gone?"

"Well, yes, of course," replied Morag, who remembered quite a few incidences of seeing things out of the corner of her eye.

"That was probably a Klapp demon," Aldiss said decisively.

Morag felt an ice-cold shiver run down her spine; she was chilled with this new knowledge.

"And how do they get about?" she asked. "Do they crawl? Do they fly? Have they got magical powers?"

"Oh, they don't have magical powers, thank goodness," said Bertie as he brought his head out from under his wing. He hated missing out on a chance to show off his knowledge. "They get about by crawling under cars and clinging on to the undercarriages," he added. "When the car drives off—with the driver completely unaware that there's a Klapp demon holding on underneath—it gets to move about the country. That's why they have such long arms and legs and really strong fingers and toes. When two cars pass, they jump from one to the other without anyone seeing. If they weren't so horrible, they would be quite fascinating creatures." He sighed. "And now one of them knows Shona is free and it will go back and tell Devlish, who will realize that Montgomery is after the Eye. He will do everything in his power to stop him. And he *will* succeed. The only advantage Montgomery has is that he might be able to take Devlish by surprise. If Devlish doesn't know he's coming, he won't be able to prepare properly. And now I've gone and ruined it."

"No you haven't," Morag said, and gave him a quick hug. "There must be *something* we can do!"

"We must warn Montgomery somehow," said Bertie. "As it's nighttime, I must call on a bat to take our message."

"But what if the Klapp demon gets to Devlish before our message?" asked Aldiss.

"We have to hope it doesn't," replied Bertie.

"How long will it take to get back to Devlish?" Morag asked, looking around at all three. Shona shrugged. Aldiss looked a bit vacant. It was Bertie who answered.

"Hmm, let me think. Well, Devlish must be en route to the WWWC AGM by now and it'll take him almost a full day to get there."

"Won't he fly?" asked Morag, who thought all witches flew on brooms.

Bertie looked at her strangely. "No," he said. "Why would you think that?"

"Hasn't he got a magic broom?"

69

"Morag, my dear, that's a myth. Witches don't fly on brooms. They fly on airplanes with humans sometimes, but they can't fly by themselves," he explained.

"Can't he just magically transport himself there?"

"No, that's too risky. Besides, he can't just magic himself into Marnoch Mor. It's not allowed. He has to go through Customs first. No, Devlish will have to travel by the humans' boat to the mainland and then by rental car, probably."

"Renting a car isn't very magical," Morag stated.

Bertie continued: "I imagine he'll arrive in Marnoch Mor late tomorrow afternoon. The Klapp demon will know he's going there and will go straight to him. If it has set off by now, it should get there around about the same time, I should think."

"So we've got tonight and most of tomorrow?" asked Morag.

"Yes, but what are you thinking?" Bertie was puzzled.

"Well," said Morag carefully, "why don't we go to Murst and get the Eye ourselves?"

Bertie, Aldiss and Shona looked at her in horror. Morag suddenly felt very uncomfortable and wished she hadn't said anything.

"We can't do that!" spluttered Bertie. "It's far too dangerous! Besides that's not what Montgomery told me to do."

"We can't wait for permission," said Morag. "We have to do something tonight! If what you've said about Devlish is true, and he keeps using the Eye, Marnoch Mor will be

70

destroyed before we know it, and then he'll use it on the rest of the world. We can't let that happen. I don't want to be a slave! We've got to do something and we've got to do it now before it's too late. If we don't, Devlish will use the Eye and it will be disastrous for all of us."

"The human is right," said Shona. "If Devlish knows Montgomery is going for the Eye, he'll do everything in his power to stop it, and that includes using darker magic against him. We don't have time to wait for Montgomery. We have to do something ourselves."

"But I must warn him nonetheless," said Bertie, looking very worried. "It'll only take a minute."

"Agreed," said the dragon. "But be quick, we don't have much time. We must leave for Murst now before Devlish returns to the island."

Bertie closed his eyes and began to chant. Within a minute, a small bat appeared in the sky and flapped around his head. Shona watched it fearfully as it landed on Bertie's shoulder. She didn't like bats either; she thought they were too much like rats with wings. She sat away from it as Bertie whispered something into the bat's little ear. When he was finished, it took off and disappeared into the dark, blustery night.

"At least now Montgomery will be warned," he said, a little bit more relaxed.

"Now that's done, let's go," said Morag. "Shona, are you fit enough to walk?"

The dragon got to her feet and stretched cautiously. She shook her head and tail like a dog does after a bath.

"Yes," she said when all the shaking was over. "I think I'll be fine."

"Okay, Shona, how do we get to Murst? Can you fly?" asked Morag.

She shook her head and smiled. "I'm not that type of dragon, I'm afraid. No, we must get to Oban, and there find the Fisherman who can take us across to Murst."

"And how do we get to Oban?" asked Morag, who was suddenly very excited at the prospect of an adventure, even though she knew it would probably be very dangerous.

"We have to go to Glasgow and travel north from there."

"But that's miles away," said Morag despairingly. "We'll *never* get there in time."

"We will if we catch the Underground," said Aldiss.

"The Underground?" said Morag, puzzled.

"Come on," he said, starting away. "If we hurry, we might catch the last train of the night."

With great effort, they helped the exhausted Shona to her feet and guided her along the uneven dune path, down the hillside and back toward the cave. Although she was quite a small dragon, it was a bit of a squeeze getting her scaly body through the mouth of the cavern. With a little pushing from behind by Morag and a heave-hoing from the front by Bertie and Aldiss, they managed to get Shona inside. Then they all stood about looking at each other and not knowing quite what to do next. Morag looked to Bertie for guidance.

"Where now?" she asked.

"I'm not quite sure," he said, and a small frown appeared

on his forehead. He put his wing up to his beak and thought hard. "I know there's an entrance here somewhere. It says so on Aldiss's map, but I can't quite remember where. It's been years since I've been in these caves—years—and even longer since I took the Underground. I wonder if it still has those pink velvet seats! They were lovely to sit on, so comfortable!"

"Bertie!" said Morag sharply. The bird jumped. "Concentrate! We don't have a lot of time, remember?"

"Oh yes, yes, quite forgot myself for a moment there." He paced up and down the cave, peering through the gloom at the cave wall. He made a lot of "hmm-ing" sounds and an occasional "Aha!," but he didn't seem to be able to find the entrance to the Underground. Shona watched him impatiently, her yellow eyes glinting in the light of the many Moonstones that lined the cave.

"Oh, hurry up, Bertie!" she cried crossly. "I'm getting cramped in here." She shifted her weight from one back leg to the other and stretched out her front legs to show him what she meant. Her scales clicked softly as she moved. Bertie nodded.

"Let me think, let me think," he muttered to himself.

"Aldiss, can't you give him a hand?" Morag asked the little rat standing at her feet. His whiskers twitched.

"No, but I can give him a paw!" he replied with a chuckle, and scampered over to where Bertie stood scratching his head. "Do you need any help, Bertie?" he asked.

"Well, I don't know if you can. I'm sure it's here somewhere. . . ."

"What is?" Aldiss and Morag asked together.

"The door handle," said Bertie sadly. "It's definitely on the wall somewhere, but I just can't find it."

"What does it look like?" asked Morag, looking around her. She expected to see a shiny brass door handle sticking out of the wall. There was none, just rock and more dust.

"Well, it's a door handle like any other," Bertie began. "Only it's made out of rock, like the rest of this cave." He patted the wall in front of him. "It's round, like an old-fashioned doorknob, but it doesn't turn. You push it and the secret door opens."

He leant against the wall. "Oh," he said in despair. "I'm afraid we'll never find it and we won't get to Murst in time to save the Eye. Oh, it's quite terrible! Oh! Deary me, deary me. Oh! Dear! OH!"

And as he leant back, a doorway suddenly opened in the cave wall. Behind it dropped a long, narrow flight of stairs. In a flurry of feathers, Bertie fell backward down the stone stairwell, which consisted of exactly thirty-one steps. He knew this because he counted as he bounced down them. Ouch! Ouch! OUCH! His friends could only watch in horror as he disappeared into the pitch-blackness. Morag ran to the doorway and anxiously peered down after him.

"Oh my goodness! Bertie!" she cried, hearing the whump of his body and his yelps as he rolled down and down and down. "Bertie! Are you all right? Bertie, can you hear me? Are you all right?"

From the depths of the earth, a tiny voice spluttered back.

"I'm fine! Come down! I think I've found the Underground!"

Scared he might be hurt, Morag wasted no time in running down into the darkness. As she slid and stumbled down the twisting stairwell, she wished she had remembered to bring a Moonstone to light her way, for the staircase was as dark as the fur of a witch's cat.

Clatter, clatter, clatter.

She could hear Shona's great claws clicking on the stone steps behind her.

Skitter, skitter, skitter.

She guessed that was the sound of Aldiss hurrying after them. On she ran, jumping two steps at a time, until suddenly she burst out into a large well-lit chamber that looked very much like the platform of any human underground train station. There were two tracks and two platforms and two tunnels on either side. The walls and the platform floor were lined with cream-colored ceramic tiles. Apart from a couple of benches, the platform was empty save for a disgruntled bird. Bertie was sitting near the door rubbing his wing. He waved when he saw her.

"Are you all right?" she asked again, and hurried to kneel beside him.

"Oh fine, fine," he answered. He winced as he tried to move. "Just a few bumps and bruises, that's all. Nothing broken except for the one feather, but I'll grow a new one, so nothing lost there," he said cheerfully. "Are the others with you?" He peered round Morag. "Ah yes, there they are."

She looked round to see the concerned faces of Shona and Aldiss looking down at them. She helped Bertie to his feet. The plump little bird's eyes watered with pain as he stood up.

"Ooh, my bottom hurts!" he complained. "My wing is sore and I bumped my head."

"Haven't you got anything for that?" asked Shona, eyeing his satchel. Bertie frowned before a look of realization dawned on his face.

"Oh yes," he said. "I almost forgot." He put a wing into the bag and pulled out a little jar of something pink. He handed it to Aldiss. "Would you mind administering this gel to my sore bits, Aldiss? Thanks awfully."

The rat took the jar reluctantly.

"Okay," he said. "But I'm not rubbing any gel onto your bottom. You can do that yourself!"

"Of course," the dodo replied.

Pheeeeeeeeeeeeeeeeeeeeeeeeeeeeeee!

A whistle rang out so loudly the four friends nearly jumped out of their skins. Then a voice that sounded as though its owner was holding his nose boomed over the loudspeaker: "The next train at platform two is the ten-thirty-five to Glasgow Green. Would passengers ensure they have all belongings and familiars."

A loud rumble resonated from the depths of the tunnel. The platform beneath their feet began to tremble, then it shook a little more and eventually the whole platform was vibrating so much they could hardly stay on their feet.

Rumble, Rumble, RUMBLE. Pheeeeeeeeeeeeeeee!

The whistle sounded again and the voice bellowed above the din: "The train now arriving at platform two is the ten-thirty-five to Glasgow Green calling at Paisley Abbey Drains, Renfrew Town Hall Back Door and The Obelisk, Glasgow Green."

Morag was beginning to feel ill from all the shaking and closed her eyes briefly until the vibrating stopped. When she opened them again, a large cream and maroon train sat at the platform. It looked very much like a train she might have caught in the world above, except that little magical-looking sparks flew from its wheels.

Shona was already moving to usher them aboard. "Come on, everyone," she said happily. She pushed a button on the side of a carriage with one of her claws and the double doors whooshed open. The dragon leapt in with a large smile on her face.

"It's been so long since I've traveled in one of these!" she called back to the others as she bounded down the carriage. Bertie and Aldiss followed her, with Morag behind.

The double doors closed behind them with a phwump, and the train carried them off.

7

By the time Morag and the others caught up with her, Shona was draped regally across two oversized squishy pink seats at the end of the carriage. She waved at them to join her. Bertie sat down next to the window, with Aldiss beside him and Morag at the end. As she sank into the marshmallowy softness of the seat, Morag thought she had never seen anything quite as strange as this train. At first glance, it looked like a normal one, but something was not quite right. Outside, the dark tunnel hurtled by, but Morag didn't want to look out the windows for too long, as she was more interested in what was around her.

The train was lit by large round stones that weren't blue like the other Moonstones, but gave off a soft milky glow.

Bertie noticed her studying them.

"Pretty, aren't they? These are Full Moonstones, and very rare," he told her. "Only the Underground has them."

The carriage looked old-fashioned to Morag, consisting of brass rails, large upholstered seats and polished dark mahogany panels on the walls. The floor looked like it was made of wooden planks, painted over with strange and colorful markings that she guessed must be magical symbols.

As she continued to look around the carriage, she began to notice more and more unusual things. The panels above the windows all carried colorful adverts. One publicized a new type of toothpaste:

"*Gleemo!* Now you too can have a bewitching smile that will dazzle your friends—and frighten nocturnal animals," the advert said. And in smaller letters it added,

"With added ghost powder for that deathly pale gleam!"

A second advert had pictures of a witch and a wizard modeling the latest in his-and-hers moleskin pointed hats. A third panel advertised special wand polish that promised to banish wand rot "for all eternity."

As she read them, Morag wondered just what she had got herself into. It had seemed like a good idea to leave Jermy and Moira and join Bertie and Aldiss on their quest, but now she wasn't so sure. She really had no idea what to expect and this realization made her a little uncomfortable, and she began to feel a tiny bit scared. It was starting to dawn on her that she may have permanently left behind everything safe and understandable for a world full of talking animals and strange dark magic. Suddenly she was afraid of the dangers she could face.

To keep herself from thinking too much about it, she craned around and looked up at the other end of the carriage.

There were only two other passengers and they were sitting several rows behind them. She knew that staring was rude, but Morag couldn't help looking at this strange pair. Not far from her was a horse, a chestnut-colored stallion sitting with his hind legs crossed one over the other. He was dressed in a gray pin-striped suit and wore a black bowler hat at a jaunty angle over one ear. In his hoofs he held open a copy of *The Supernatural Times*. Every now and then, he snorted with derision at something he was reading and obviously didn't agree with.

A few seats further away was something that resembled a woman with long black hair knotted like a clutch of seaweed. She had piercing black eyes and scowled at Morag when she caught her looking. There was something strangely beautiful about her and normally Morag would not have gawped at all, but she couldn't help herself—the woman's skin was sea green and dripping with water.

"Morag!" Shona whispered, breaking Morag's concentration. She jumped at the sound of her name and quickly looked round at the dragon.

"Stop staring at that kelpie, you'll have her over here in a minute and then there'll be trouble. They are notoriously bad-tempered creatures, they are. Have your eyes out in a minute, so they would," warned the dragon.

"Sorry, it's just that I've never seen one before," she muttered, giving Shona a weak smile. She tried to look out the window, but the sight of the kelpie was too interesting and before long Morag found herself peering at the beautiful creature again.

The kelpie was still glaring at her, and bared her serrated teeth in a growl. Shocked, Morag quickly lowered her eyes and looked away. She didn't want to irritate this water creature, as there was no knowing what she might do. Before now, Morag had had no idea such peculiar, dangerous people existed, and she decided it was probably safer to try and read some of the letters painted on the floor. Looking down at the boards, she saw that the curious letters had been worn away under their feet and soon she got bored of looking at her spot, so she searched for a more interesting piece of floor.

Just then, her attention was caught by the sight of a large white bear in a smart blue conductor's uniform making his way down the carriage. His brass buttons shone as he walked slowly down the aisle. Over a shoulder he carried his metal ticket machine in a leather bag.

"Tickets from Irvine, please!" the polar bear shouted as he came closer.

Morag looked at the others with concern. They didn't have any tickets. She began to feel a bit edgy and saw that Bertie was rummaging frantically in his bag. His face squirmed and frowned and grimaced as he searched for something that was proving to be elusive. Then, with a satisfied smile, he drew out a little leather pouch. He emptied it onto his outstretched wing and four large gold coins tumbled out onto his gray feathers just as the bear approached.

"Tickets, please!" the polar bear said sharply.

"Four tickets to Oban McCaig's Tower via Glasgow Green Obelisk," said Bertie, offering the coins.

The bear took them grumpily, slipped them into his pocket and pulled his ticket machine from its bag. He wound the handle and four pink tickets reeled off. He tore them from the strip and handed them to Bertie.

"Have a nice trip," he growled before turning and lumbering back down the carriage.

Bertie held on to the tickets with one wing while Morag looked at them with curiosity. There was something strangely familiar about them.

"Can I have a look at those tickets?" she asked. The dodo handed them over.

They fit perfectly in the palm of her hand. She looked at them closely. Each cardboard ticket was small and pink and had destinations printed in little black letters. Morag looked round at her friends. They were deep in conversation and didn't notice her pull a little red book from her housecoat pocket, open it and take out a tiny slip of pink cardboard from between its pages. She held the slip in one hand and the new tickets in the other. They were identical. She quickly put her old ticket back into her book and slipped it back into the safety of her pocket. The tickets are the same, she thought. How can that be?

She fixed her eyes on the floor, her mind racing with possibilities as she searched for an answer. She thought long and hard, but no sensible answer came. She could not think how a ticket for the magical Underground could have found its way into the possession of her parents. Her head began to hurt and she looked around her, searching for something else to think about.

As she did, something shiny caught her eye. Something gold and glittering lay under Shona's seat, next to the point of her tail. Morag got up and knelt down. She put her hand under the chair and felt along the floor. Shona, who had been chatting to Bertie about the best way to roast asparagus, jumped in fright.

"What are you doing?" she asked nervously. She lifted her claws as Morag crawled under the chair.

"Morag? MORAG!" But Morag was too busy reaching for the glimmering object. It was almost within her reach. She stretched as far as she could and . . .

"Got it!" she said, and emerged from under the seat with a large golden disc attached to a long chain. She held it up triumphantly as her friends stared at it in curiosity.

"What is it?" Aldiss asked, his little black eyes glittering in the light of the Full Moonstones.

"Some sort of necklace?" Morag mused aloud as she held it up for a better look.

It was indeed some sort of necklace. A medallion to be exact, and a very beautiful one at that. The edges were encrusted with glittering pink and yellow diamonds and in the center was a round flat disc etched with small, almost-not-there markings that could have been a nose, a mouth and two little eyes.

Morag squinted and angled it toward the light. She was sure she could make out an indistinct face. As she stared, one of the eyes seemed to wink. She pulled back in alarm. The others didn't notice, and continued to speculate.

"I wonder how it got under there?" said Shona.

"Someone must have lost it," said Aldiss.

"Who could have done that?" said Bertie, mesmerized by its beauty. "It looks awfully valuable."

"It is!" cried a shrill voice from down the carriage. They all turned to see a thin woman wearing a long black velvet coat trimmed with fluffy red marabou feathers and shiny gold buttons striding up to them. "Ah, there he is! I've been looking for him everywhere. He must have slipped off when I wasn't looking."

"Him?" repeated the four friends in unison. They stared at the woman questioningly.

"Yes," she said as she swept up to them and put out a slim hand. Morag pulled away before she could grab the medallion from her. The woman looked annoyed.

"Yes, *him*," she said, nodding at it. "Henry," she added, as if they ought to know who she meant.

"Who is Henry?" asked Bertie.

"*This* is Henry," the woman said, and pointed to the medallion. Morag looked at it. Surely she didn't mean . . .

"Yes, this!" the woman insisted, her voice becoming exasperated. "This is Hieronymus Algernon. I call him Henry. He's perfectly house-trained, but has a habit of going missing, don't you, Henry?"

Everyone turned to look at the medallion in Morag's

hand. It didn't move and didn't speak. It didn't even wink, no matter how hard Morag stared at it this time. The woman took another step forward.

"And I'll have him back now, thank you," she said, holding out her hand expectantly.

Initially Morag was too stunned to react, but then she came to her senses. She held the medallion away from the woman.

"How do I know it's yours?" she asked defiantly, staring at the woman's startled face.

"Of course he's mine, you silly girl," she replied stiffly. "Who *else* would have him?"

"How dare you say that!" a tinny voice sounded from somewhere, no, not somewhere, but from Morag's hand.

With a shriek of fright, she dropped it on the floor and it rolled back under Shona's seat.

"Ouch!" the medallion cried out loudly. "Does everyone have to keep dropping me?"

"Oh, oh, my poor baby!" screeched the woman. She fell to her knees and groped under the seat. "Come here, Henry, come on, be a darling and don't roll away from Mummy. Ouch! Henry! What have I said about biting?"

Morag stared in disbelief. Talking, biting jewelry doesn't exist, does it? she wondered. After everything else that had happened today, she was no longer sure. She looked at Aldiss, who crossed his eyes and twirled his finger next to his ear to suggest he thought the woman was mad. Morag laughed out loud. The sound of her giggles caught the woman's attention and she emerged from under the seat, lips pursed and the medallion dangling jauntily from her hand.

"And what are you laughing at?" she asked crossly as she smoothed her tousled hair with her free hand. "Eh?"

She looked straight at Morag, who suddenly felt embarrassed and shifted uncomfortably.

"Nothing," the girl muttered, and stared at the floor.

"She was laughing at you, you stupid woman!" the medallion said crossly. "Now give me back to her! I've told you before I'm not staying with you. I'm going to make my own way in the world now—without you. I'm fed up being worn at your crummy séances and amateurish coven meetings. And as for that stupid cat of yours! If it lifts its leg on me one more time, I'm going to blast it into its ninth life. I'm bored, I'm underused and I quit! I want to see more of the world, not be stuck with a cat with a piddling problem and its silly-haired witch!"

Now it was the woman's turn to look uncomfortable. Her white face turned crimson with embarrassment as she said, "You know quite well that Noodles is getting on in years and can't help himself. And I don't have silly hair. It's all the rage in Paris!"

"When?" snapped the medallion. "When you lot lived in caves?"

The woman gasped. She gave the others a weak smile before turning on the medallion. She held it up to her face and gave it her best frown.

"Henry!" she shouted. "We will speak about this later. For now, you're going back in your box where you'll stay until I've got time to have words with you. Now thank the nice people for finding you."

The medallion stayed sullenly quiet. She shook it violently, causing it to swing at Shona's face, who pulled back just in time before it could hit her.

"I said, say thank you!" spat the woman, eyes bright with fury. In fact, Morag was horrified to see they had started to glow the color of lava. She took a step away. The woman shook the medallion more violently. It swung out of control and narrowly missed Aldiss and Bertie, who both yelped in surprise.

The medallion said nothing.

"Well, if that's how you want it, that's fine. You can just stay in my pocket and I'll deal with you later." The woman sniffed and stuffed the silent medallion into a large pocket before turning to the shocked foursome.

Composing herself into a more agreeable mood, she gave them each a little nod before saying: "Thank you so much for finding my Henry. I'm most grateful, and I'm terribly sorry about his rude behavior. You can be sure I will speak to him later. I promise you he will be severely reprimanded about this. Anyway, we must go, we're getting off at the next stop."

With a snippy "Thank you!" she spun about on the high heels of her boots and marched to the double doors of the carriage. As she waited for the train to pull into the next station, she tapped her foot impatiently on the floor. Tap, tap, tap, it went. Tap, tap, tap.

Morag and her new friends stared at her openmouthed.

They each felt like they had been hit by a hurricane at full force. Morag returned to her seat next to Aldiss.

"What do you make of *that*?" he whispered.

He looked back fearfully, afraid the dreadful woman was listening.

"I've never seen anything like that in my life!" Morag said quietly.

The train slowed and from the carriage speaker system, a voice boomed out: "The train is now approaching Paisley Abbey Drains. The train is now approaching Paisley Abbey Drains."

Now the woman stopped tapping her foot and straightened herself. The train stopped, the doors slid open and she stepped off without looking back.

The friends watched as, face serious and tight-lipped, she strode past their window and quickly disappeared up some stairs to the world above. They all sighed with relief.

"Thank goodness that strange woman has gone," said Bertie. "I'm so relieved she's not going as far as Glasgow Green, I don't think I could have taken much more of her."

"Tell me about it!" said a familiar tinny voice. Everyone turned toward Morag, for the voice had come from her direction. She looked as shocked and puzzled as her friends. She shrugged to say she didn't know where it was coming from either.

"Magma has a warm heart, but she can talk for Scotland," continued the voice. "After a while it got so wearing."

"I think," said Shona, pointing at Morag's housecoat, "there's a voice coming from your pocket!"

Fearful that whatever was in there would bite her, Morag slid her hand into her pocket carefully. Her fingers touched something large, round and cold. Slowly she pulled it out by the chain.

"Hellooooo!" cried Henry theatrically. "Guess who?"

"Oh my goodness!" said Morag, and her free hand flew to her mouth in surprise. "How did you get in there?" She peered at him and saw he was clearly smiling. Quite smugly, as it happened.

"Is that how you normally greet a new friend?" said Henry. "Nice to see you all again! Oh, what a relief to be rescued from that awful woman!" He paused and stared expectantly at Morag.

She didn't know what to do and looked to her friends for help, but they didn't know what to do either.

"So," continued Henry, "are you going to introduce me to yourself and your friends? You look like you might be going somewhere interesting. That's why I chose you. Where are you going? You can tell me! Go on!"

Morag didn't know what to say. She was so surprised she felt her tongue was frozen in her head.

"Well, you'll make a change from that other one. I couldn't get a word in," said the medallion.

The carriage speaker system voice announced they had arrived at Renfrew Town Hall Back Door. Henry ignored the announcement and continued to talk.

"We'll start with something simple. My name is Henry, and your name is . . . ?"

"Morag," replied Morag.

"Good. There you go! How difficult was that?" he replied. "Turn me around so I can look at your friends while they're introduced to me. Come on, chop-chop. Turn me around, girl."

Morag held the medallion up by the chain, like a hypnotist, as her equally bemused friends introduced themselves to it one by one.

"So," it said when everyone had finished. "Where are you going? I know, I know! Don't tell me! You're looking for something?" His tiny eyes gleamed with pleasure. "Am I right?"

"Well . . . ," began Morag.

"Don't tell me! Let me guess!" continued the medallion. "You're going to Glasgow Green?"

"You're right about that," said Aldiss. He was shushed by Bertie, who glared at him.

"What?" asked the rat. "He would have seen where we got off the train!"

"No, it's good to be discreet, isn't it? So, I guess that you're going to Glasgow Green to look for something?"

"No," said Morag.

"Oh!" Henry sounded disappointed. "Then where are you really going?"

"We have to catch another train. We're on some very important business," she began, unable to take her eyes off him.

"Be careful, Morag!" Shona warned.

"But what that business is, is none of your business," Bertie interrupted officiously as Henry opened his mouth to speak again.

"It doesn't matter," said the medallion. "I can tell that you're going north and that you want to keep your whereabouts a secret."

"You're not coming," preempted Bertie.

"What?" scoffed the medallion. "Not coming? Of course I am. I didn't leave Magma to end up in a provincial Lost and Found office. I'm in search of adventure just like you, and I chose you because I know where you're headed, so of course I'm coming!"

Bertie gave Henry his very best withering look and sighed.

"Listen," he said. "Firstly, we didn't ask you to join us—you invited yourself. Secondly, we don't need anyone else to come with us, thank you very much. And thirdly, the Lost and Found office is exactly where you're going. That way you can be safely reunited with your rightful owner, Miss, er . . . What's-Her-Face!"

The medallion said nothing for a moment and looked at Bertie blankly. Then he grimaced and began to breathe very slowly and very loudly as if he were calming his temper, his little gold cheeks puffing in and out, in and out.

"Who made *you* captain?" he finally asked. "I've chosen you and that's that. Besides, Magma wasn't my owner. She was in a sense my vehicle. I needed her to get me here, but I was stuck with her for too long. No, dear feather face, you and your friends are my new friends and there's nothing you can do about it!"

"Feather face?" spluttered Bertie. "Take that back, you nickel-plated novelty!"

"Gentlemen, focus!" It was Shona's turn to speak.

Bertie and the medallion looked round at the dragon. "Let's not fight," she continued. "Henry, my friend is right, we don't need another—er—person on this trip, but thank you very much anyway."

The medallion's tiny face slid into melancholy.

"I would be an asset," Henry said. "I can do things that might come in handy."

Morag looked closely at the medallion. "What kind of things?" she asked suspiciously.

"I can make the person wearing me invisible," he said. "I'm good at finding things and I can speak forty-two languages, including Klapp demon and Lurgy."

"I have to admit it, that could be very useful," said Shona thoughtfully. She looked round at her fellow travelers. "Morag, my dear, could you put Henry down while we discuss this? That's okay, isn't it, Henry?"

"Oh yes," said Henry, suddenly very keen to be nice in the hope they would allow him to come.

So Morag laid the medallion on an empty seat several rows away and returned to her friends. Bertie was looking very cheesed off, Aldiss had a vacant look in his eyes as if he were daydreaming about whatever rats daydream of, but Shona got down to business straightaway as the four of them huddled together.

"I think I know that medallion," she whispered. "I heard of him before I was turned to stone. If I'm right, he's quite powerful, magically. He could be very useful in the days ahead."

"I'm not convinced," replied Bertie grumpily. "We

can't just trust anyone. What if he's a spy? By taking him along, he could lead us straight into Devlish's hands. We could end up captured and thrown in a dungeon for all eternity. Look what Devlish did to you, Shona."

"I'd like to try out that invisibility thing, it could be fun!" said Aldiss. "If only I were invisible, I'd run into the biggest cheese factory and eat everything in sight and no one could stop me!" He giggled, but stopped when he realized no one else was laughing.

"What do you think, Morag?" asked Shona.

Morag turned back to the medallion, gleaming in the light of the Moonstones. She could hear him humming to himself over the sound of the train's engine.

"I'm not sure either." She frowned. "Part of me agrees with Bertie." Beside her the bird puffed his gray feathers with pride. "And another part of me agrees with you because we could use all the help we can get."

The others nodded, and Shona said, "We'd better make up our minds before that kelpie over there gets ahold of him. She's been eyeing him since you laid him there."

They turned to look, and sure enough the kelpie was looking over with avid interest at the glittering medallion on the seat. She got to her feet and began to move down the carriage toward him, water dripping from her long black hair, leaving a trail along the passage. Morag felt a wave of panic rise in her stomach.

"I say we take him with us," she said quickly.

"Me too," Aldiss squeaked.

"Agreed," said Shona.

Only Bertie had to vote. He hesitated.

"I'm still not sure," he said.

"Bertie!" they all cried in exasperation.

"All right." He sighed. "But at the first sign of trouble, he's out."

"Absolutely," said Morag.

The kelpie was just reaching out for the medallion when Morag sprinted down the passageway and swept him up in her hand.

"This is mine," said Morag, staring into the kelpie's jet-black eyes. Those beautiful eyes narrowed with anger, and the kelpie raised a hand as if to strike Morag. Shona rose up behind the girl and bared her teeth. The kelpie saw the dragon and immediately lowered her hand. She hissed at Morag, her breath smelling of stagnant rockpools, and slowly retreated to her seat, mumbling to herself all the way.

"That was close," said Henry. "Didn't fancy living in the water myself; wouldn't have done much for the old gold work. So, have you made a decision?"

Morag held him up so she could see his face.

"Yes, we'd like you to join us." She smiled.

"You won't regret this," he replied.

"I sincerely hope not," muttered Bertie.

Morag and Shona went back to their seats while the medallion continued talking about what a real asset he would be to the group.

"And I'm great company, I know some very good stories," he continued.

Bertie sighed. "Henry!" he said sharply. The tone of his voice jolted the medallion into silence.

"Yes, feather face?" he said innocently.

"Please stop talking!"

"Okay, feather face."

"And let's get two things clear," the dodo went on. "Firstly, you are on probation. One wrong move and you're being deposited in the nearest kelpie's sea-purse. And secondly, my name is Bertie, not 'feather face.' Is that understood?"

"Loud and clear, feather face," replied the medallion, before he was thrown from Morag's hand into Bertie's lap.

The train had stopped suddenly.

They had arrived at their destination: The Obelisk at Glasgow Green.

8

The train ground to a sudden halt at the Underground station. Through the window, Morag saw a sign saying THE OBELISK, GLASGOW GREEN. She put Henry round her neck and followed the others as they each jumped off the carriage.

Once on the wide platform, Morag was puzzled by the way her friends were acting; they were all looking around as if they were searching for something. Aldiss, in particular, was scurrying across the platform having a thorough sniff of the ornate wooden benches, where passengers sat waiting for their trains. He sniffed the large billboard advertising "Instant Familiars! Add three drops of a Siren's tears and within seconds you're the proud owner of a fantastic new witch's cat. Guaranteed for a year." He sniffed a disgruntled Bertie, who whacked him on his little rat snout for having such gall. He sniffed the air and found only the musty smell of the Underground.

"What are we looking for?" asked Morag after Aldiss gave her boots a good sniff. Looking around her, all she could see was another Underground platform, albeit a larger one, lit by Full Moonstones.

"Train time information," said Bertie. "I don't know if it'll be here or upstairs. Hold on a minute and I'll go and look."

Without another word, the dodo hurried over to a set of stairs that had a big sign next to it saying UP and a large gold arrow pointing skyward. He began to climb and soon disappeared into the dark, leaving the others wondering what was going on.

"Are we going to catch another train?" Morag asked Aldiss. She thought he would most likely know because he had been with Bertie since the beginning.

"Dunno," replied the rat. "Maybe." He shrugged. "Bertie hasn't told me."

"What do you know, Shona?" Morag asked the dragon.

"Everything is new to me too at the moment!" She laughed and shook her great head. Then Bertie reappeared at the bottom of the stairs.

"This way," he said, waving them over. "I know where we're going now. Follow me upstairs."

And with that, he began to climb again. Shona bounded after him, with Aldiss scrambling behind, followed by

Morag with Henry, who was muttering about people not knowing what they were doing and how dangerous that could be.

Each step took them further into darkness, which was lit only by the occasional flaming torch, and Morag began to feel a little afraid as she climbed.

Another steep set of stairs followed the one before, and they were all puffing and panting by the time they reached the top. Bertie put his shoulder against the wall and pushed. A doorway opened up. The flood of light caused them to screw up their eyes and hold their hands to their faces for protection.

Once her eyes were accustomed to the light again, Morag saw they were at the entrance to an enormous cavern, brightly lit and busy. Ahead of them were seven train platforms. A large screen near the rafters was being drawn and redrawn by small winged creatures to tell passengers where trains were going and what times they would be departing. There were shops selling everything from birds' nests and restorative cures to fairy snacks and amulets. And as they passed him, a small, ugly man standing at a green-and-gold-colored stall called out, "Top-quality second-hand magical pets! All fully trained in the obscure and domestic arts!" And on his stall, in a range of different sized wicker cages, sat a loose assortment of unamused black cats, owls, toads and one large hairy spider.

Morag looked around in amazement. It wasn't just the appearance of the place that surprised her, but the amount of strange and wonderful-looking people wandering about the station. Witches and wizards were staring up at the screen, searching for their trains. All kinds of animals dressed in cloaks and hats and boots chatted amiably to each other, or drank coffee and tea out of polystyrene cups. On one platform she noticed a white unicorn in a cocktail dress and diamanté earrings being helped with her cases.

"Wow," gasped Morag as three gryphons dressed in white shorts and red hooded tops jogged past bearing a banner saying: *U.K. Station Charity Challenge in aid of The Marnoch Mor Magic Folk's Retirement Home*. "This place is amazing."

"Isn't it?" agreed Bertie, who hadn't noticed the gryphons. "It was opened two hundred years ago, you know, and it's never been shut. Beautiful architecture. Just look at that ceiling!"

Morag looked up and saw a vaulted marble ceiling painted with beautiful scenes from (as Bertie told her) Marnoch Mor mythology. The dodo had just begun to tell her more about the pictures when he was interrupted by a loudspeaker announcement.

"The next train for Oban leaves from platform seven, calling at: Arrochar Old Kirk, Tyndrum Post Box, Falls of Cruachan (Under), Taynuilt Signal Box and McCaig's Tower, Oban," said the announcer.

"Speckled hens!" cried the dodo, all feathers and fluster. "I was so busy talking I nearly forgot we have another train to catch. Come on, we must hurry or we'll miss it."

"Another underground train?" Morag said, who had quite enjoyed the last journey.

"No, no," said the dodo, trotting away toward platform seven. "This time we're going on an over-underground train. It's quite different. Still underground, but not so deep under the ground and sometimes it comes up for air. Come on, come on, follow me, or we'll miss it."

The girl, the dodo, the rat and the dragon ran through the busy station, dodging fellow passengers and a man selling something called "Wot Dogs" from a stall. With seconds to spare, they each managed to get on the over-underground train, and before they could even take a seat, the doors closed with a decisive swish and the train started to pull out of the station.

Sweating and panting, the four found themselves in a small curtained compartment furnished with high-backed ornate seats covered in deep blue velvet. Morag turned on a small lamp on a short table under the window and looked around with Aldiss, as the other two made themselves comfortable. With a claw Shona pulled back the curtain and looked out. "How long is the journey?" she asked.

"A good two or three hours," Bertie informed her.

"I don't think I can stay awake for much longer," she said. "All that running around after being still for so long takes its toll on someone my age!"

Aldiss found some woolen blankets folded up on the luggage rack and brought them down. "Maybe it's time we all had a nap," he suggested.

"I couldn't agree more," said Bertie as Morag unfolded a blanket for him. "I want us all to be bright-eyed and bushy-tailed by the time we reach Oban," he said, nestling down. "We won't get there until sometime after midnight.

And we may have a long night ahead of us. So, good night all, and sweet dreams."

And with that, the dodo tucked his head under his wing and closed his eyes. Soon there were snoring sounds coming from underneath his feathers and strange little noises, which sounded as if he was talking in his sleep. Morag smiled. Silly old bird, she thought fondly.

Morag pulled the blanket around her and watched Aldiss and Shona close their eyes drowsily. She was quite exhausted from all the excitement of the day and didn't know how she could stay awake either. Her eyes were heavy with sleep, her body aching from all the crawling and running, and she felt that if she could just get a half an hour of sleep she would feel much better.

Oh, she thought, looking at her friends being rocked to sleep in the soft light, this is so lovely, I could stay here forever . . . and then she remembered nothing more, for she was fast asleep.

It was Henry who woke them. It was Henry who alerted them to the fact they had arrived. If it hadn't been for Henry, they probably would have continued sleeping and stayed on the train until it turned round and went back to Glasgow.

"Oh, for goodness' sake, will you lot wake up!" he said crossly. He had been trying to rouse them for more than ten minutes and was getting thoroughly fed up. Morag forced her eyes open and glanced down at the medallion around her neck. Henry was frowning, but smiled when he saw Morag was awake.

"We've arrived," he announced.

She sat up, yawned, stretched and pulled aside the curtain to look out of the window. Sure enough, the train had come to a halt at a brick-built Victorian station, the kind with flower baskets hanging from the decorative white wooden struts under the eaves and a fat red clay chimney pot. Morag looked closer. There was something not quite right about this, she knew, but she wasn't exactly sure why. Then a large owl in a stationmaster's uniform appeared at the window. He blinked. She blinked. He raised a whistle to his lips and blew.

Peeeeeee-wheeeeeeeeeeeeeeeeeee!

It was the loudest whistle Morag had ever heard and the shrill, eerie screech made the slumbering Shona, Bertie and Aldiss waken with a jolt. Aldiss whimpered with fright.

"Well, *that* got your attention!" said Henry smugly, and sniggered quietly to himself.

Still dopey with sleep, the four friends got to their feet and walked stiffly off the train onto the little platform and into a light mist of rain. A large white sign bolted onto the wall of the station building told them they had arrived at McCaig's Tower in Oban. Rubbing their eyes, they gathered beneath the sign and waited until someone took charge.

"Ah! *That's* what it was!" said Morag a little too loudly, making everyone jump.

"That's what *what* was?" asked Shona, yawning lazily.

"I was trying to work out what was different about this station," she said. "And I have."

"Well?" said Bertie a little tetchily. He was stiff and

sore from sleeping in an uncomfortable position for hours. He was also very hungry. "Spit it out, girl."

"We're outside," Morag said, taking a deep breath of the cold night air.

It felt good to feel the wind on her face again after hours being underground. They looked around them, and sure enough, they were standing on a platform at a little station in the middle of nowhere in the open air, except it wasn't quite in the middle of nowhere, because all around them were the tall narrow stone arches of an unfinished and open-roofed circular wall. Morag, who had seen pictures of this place before, knew they were in the middle of Oban's most memorable landmark: McCaig's Tower. The only difference was that in the pictures she had seen in books, there had not been a small station and railway track, and she momentarily wondered how the magic folk had managed to keep it so well hidden.

Something nudged at her feet and she looked down to see a small poster had blown onto the platform. She picked it up and examined it under the dull lights of the station. Morag gasped—there was a picture of her on it!

"Missing: Ten-year-old Morag, from Stoker's Sea View Guesthouse, Irvine. Small for age. Take care when approaching—tendency to violence. If you've seen her, call Jermy and Moira Stoker at Irvine Police Station."

She quickly screwed up the paper and stuffed it in her pocket. They were looking for her.

"Are you all right, Morag?" Bertie asked.

"Yes, fine, thanks," she replied quickly.

It was still pitch-black and they could see very little beyond the lights of the station except for the tall walls of the tower and the tiny twinkling lights of the seaside town below. It was, however, very cold and the wind was getting up again. Morag shivered, and drew her housecoat closer. Shona was also feeling the cold. Her tail was trembling and her great big sharp teeth were chittering in the autumn night air.

"Whhhhheeeerrrree tooooo nnnnnow?" she asked Bertie. "And cccccan we ggggo somewwwwhere warm for a bbbbbowl of ssssssoup or ssssomething? I'm frrrrrreezing."

Bertie looked at all his friends shivering there before him and nodded.

"Agreed. I know of a splendid little establishment not far from here," he said.

His stomach growled loudly and he winced with embarrassment. Ignoring the mad noises, he stuck a wing into his bag and pulled out a large ticking clock. The numerals glowed a luminous green and showed that the time was nearly two o'clock in the morning.

He sighed. "I hope it's still open. If it's not, we'll just have to make do with whatever the satchel can come up with," he added, patting his bag fondly.

"Can't we do that just now?" Aldiss asked. "I'm starving too!"

"We could, but wouldn't it be better to eat something hot inside a nice snug restaurant?" said Bertie wisely. "And we might be able to get a bed for the rest of the night."

"Oh, that sounds lovely," Morag said dreamily, wishing she were in bed already.

"Right then," replied Bertie. "That settles it. Follow me."

Eleanor's Excellent Eatery was a short walk down the hill from the station. It was perched on a mound overlooking the town, and Morag wondered how she had not spotted it from the rail track, but decided not to question anyone about it. She supposed, rightly, that the café was protected by some kind of magic that made it difficult for humans to see or find.

As it was mainly made of glass, the restaurant looked like an overgrown conservatory. Candle-filled lanterns glowed cheerily at the windows, and peeking through the cracks in the heavy red curtains, Morag saw three or four customers inside enjoying huge bowls of soup and large steaming platters of meat covered in gravy.

Now it was *her* stomach's turn to growl. She licked her lips in anticipation and followed Bertie and the others inside.

It was heaven to be inside a warm and cozy place like Eleanor's. As tired and as weary as she was, Morag was really looking forward to ordering a huge bowl of hot soup with a chunk of warm crusty bread dripping with melted butter.

Bertie took them inside, to a table close to the huge log fire at the back. Once they had settled down, they had a look at the menu.

Morag could hardly believe her eyes at the amount of

tempting dishes that were on offer and suddenly her big bowl of soup didn't seem so appealing. All her favorite meals were there and she had a hard time choosing between macaroni and cheese, fish pie with seasonal vegetables or mince, mashed potatoes and baked beans. In the end, she opted for the macaroni and wasn't disappointed with her choice when the waitress, a little old lady with shuffling feet, brought over a huge plate of pasta smothered in a three-cheese sauce. She tucked in hungrily.

"So," said the old lady when she had put the final plate down in front of her new guests and handed each a piping hot mug of cocoa on the house. "Will you be wanting a bed for the night?"

She had a strange lisping accent and a nervy manner. Morag looked at her curiously. There was something about this woman that unsettled her, but she didn't know why.

The little old lady looked like a lot of little old ladies she had seen: white hair permed into tight curls, no makeup and oversized glasses that hung on a chain around her neck. She wore a gray woolen skirt and a fine-knit top and matching cardigan. On her feet, she had shapeless granny shoes. She looked quite harmless, but for some reason Morag didn't trust her.

And then there was the man she noticed in the corner. He was dressed in a fine purple cloak and kept looking over at them. He was hunched over a bowl of something that looked like porridge. Hood up, his brooding eyes were all that Morag could see glinting in the firelight. She tried not to look at him, tried not to catch his eye, but every time she looked up, there he was, looking directly back at her.

"Yes, we would," said Bertie, answering the old lady's question. He spooned a mouthful of muesli into his beak.

"How many would that be now? Four rooms, or would ye share?" she asked him. "I've got a very nice room up top that would suit three of you and another room for the young lady here."

"That would be fine," decided Bertie, his beak still full of raisins. "You can show us the way after we've finished," he said, then added hastily, "If you don't mind, please."

The old woman shrugged. "I don't mind at all. You'll be paying the same money!"

When she shuffled away in the direction of the kitchen, Morag was glad to see her leave.

"Listen," Morag whispered. "Can I say something that's been troubling me?"

Bertie furrowed his brow. He was too exhausted for "something troubling," but didn't want to be rude. He sighed.

"Go on," he said cautiously.

"Well," said Morag quietly, looking around. The man in the corner was gazing directly at her again. He smiled knowingly when he realized she was looking at him. She shivered. "It's this place. Is it just me or do any of you feel strange?" she whispered.

"What do you mean by 'strange'?" asked Shona, with her mouth full of steak pie and pickles. She too looked around her.

"I don't know. I don't feel safe here," hissed Morag. "I can't put my finger on it. I'm probably just being silly, aren't I?" She plunged her fork into the remainder of her macaroni and scooped up a forkful.

"Not safe? Not safe?" said Aldiss hesitantly.

"Why, my dear, you're perfectly safe with us," said Bertie. "Don't you worry. You're probably just feeling tired, that's all. It will all seem better in the morning."

"I hope so," she replied. She yawned. She was looking forward to getting to bed.

"Psssssssst!" It was Henry. Morag looked down to the medallion. "Morag," he said, "you'll be fine. I'll watch out for us all."

"Thanks, Henry." She smiled, but something made her uneasy and she still didn't feel entirely comforted.

She looked over to where the man was sitting. A giant of a woman whose face and body were obscured by a hooded black woolen cloak had joined him now. The two were deep in conversation, but that didn't prevent the man from looking over once more. Morag's heart missed a beat. She longed to be away from this restaurant.

After the meal, the old woman showed them to two rooms at the top of the building. They climbed three flights of stairs on the glass side of the building and were all feeling quite exhausted by the end.

The old woman unlocked the first door with an ancient iron key and pushed it open. The door creaked eerily. She handed Morag a candlestick in which sat a wavering candle.

"Here you are, little one," she said with a slight smile. "I hope you sleep well," she added meaningfully. Then she leant toward the others.

"Follow me, you're all next door. In the bigger room," she said, showing them a second iron key that she slipped into the lock of the door of the room adjacent to Morag's. "Here we are. I hope you're all comfortable," she said, opening the door and ushering Shona, Bertie and Aldiss in-side. "If there's nothing else, I'll say good night."

Without another word, she turned on her heel and shuffled down the corridor to the stairs. As she passed, Morag felt a chill go down her spine. She didn't like this place one bit, but was too tired to do anything but go to bed. Still holding the candlestick, she hesitated at the door.

"I suppose we had all better turn in," Morag began, not looking forward to the prospect of being in the room on her own. "Good night, Bertie, Aldiss and Shona!"

"Good night, Morag," Aldiss called back.

"Sleep well," said Shona.

"Sweet dreams," Bertie replied.

Morag went inside and shut the door. It was a small plain room with a comfortable-looking bed in the corner and a little bedside cabinet. Too tired to take off her clothes, she pulled off her boots and slipped under the covers. As she began to lift Henry from around her neck, he spoke up suddenly.

"Stop, leave me where I am," he said kindly. "I'll pro-tect you from whatever's bothering you."

"That's just it," whispered Morag. "I don't know what is bothering me. I should feel fine. The journey here was nice, the food downstairs was good, and now this bed is comfortable. So why do I still feel afraid? Am I being silly?"

"Not at all," replied the medallion. "It must be difficult for someone like you, coming from the land of men. Of course you're bound to feel frightened. All this must seem very strange."

"You're probably right. Thanks, Henry," Morag said, putting her head on the soft pillow. She felt for her book in her pocket and was comforted by its hard shape against her body. Before she could even say good night to her new protector, she fell fast asleep.

"Good night, Morag," said the medallion softly.

Next door, the dodo, the dragon and the rat were deciding which of the three large beds they wanted to sleep in. As Bertie and Shona argued over which to take, their bickering was stopped short by a brown blur rushing past them and squeaking, "Bagsy me the bed by the window!"

While they had wasted time quarreling, Aldiss had secured himself the best one. The dragon and the dodo stared at him, stunned by his audacity. Shona shrugged and leapt onto the nearest bed. Bertie took the remaining one. Some plumping of pillows took place, some snuggling and soon there was silence. A snort and a snore indicated that both Bertie and Shona were quickly fast asleep. There was no sound from Aldiss, but he was curled up in a tight ball under the covers of his bed.

They knew nothing more until morning.

9

It was all done very quickly, and very efficiently. No one knew anything was amiss until late the next morning when Morag didn't answer Shona's knock at her door. The dragon, thinking she was still asleep, carefully turned the handle and peeped round the door. The curtains were still drawn and the bed, ruffled from where Morag had slept, was unmade. The rest of the room was still and tidy, but there was no sign of the girl, or her medallion. Even Morag's green Wellington boots were gone.

Shona left the room and went back to tell the other two. Bertie was sitting on his bed preening his feathers and Aldiss was doing some stretching exercises on the floor. They both looked up as she entered.

111

"They're not there," said Shona, with concern in her voice.

"Perhaps they've already gone down to breakfast," Aldiss suggested, doing a final back stretch.

Bertie, who was feeling quite cheerful that morning, was just as optimistic.

"That's where they'll be, all right!" he said. "That girl will be starving; they always are at that age. She'll have gone down early and will be tucking into something tasty as we speak." His little pink tongue licked his beak as he said this, as he thought about breakfast.

"But why didn't they wake us?" Shona asked, with her face creased into a frown.

"Because they knew we were tired and needed to sleep on a bit," replied the dodo. "I'll bet Morag is downstairs right now filling up with fresh baked bread or pancakes!"

He pushed himself off the bed and stood before Shona, with his wings on his hips. "And, dear Shona," he concluded, slinging his satchel over his shoulder, "I, for one, am going down to join them." And with a flurry of gray feathers, he walked out of the room.

"Me too!" Aldiss squeaked, running after his friend. "Wait for me!" He scuttled out the door in Bertie's wake. The dodo was already descending the stairs when Aldiss caught up, and together, they went down for breakfast, leaving Shona behind in their room.

The dragon had a bad feeling about Morag and Henry. She went back to Morag's room and had a second look for clues. The room looked just as it had before, with nothing to make her suspicious, so she could think of nothing else but to follow her friends down to the restaurant to see if the girl and medallion were indeed there.

She caught up with Bertie and Aldiss as they were reading a large blackboard at the entrance to the restaurant. On it was chalked "Today's Specials" and a list of peculiar food—Eleanor's Human-Style Special; Wartsproggit Eyes in Tomato Sauce; Whimsical Porridge with Fairy Ice Cream; and Glooglop Eggs on Lava Bread Toast. Taped to the board was a sheet of paper marked "Extra Specials!" and this included Fried Wot Dogs with Mushrooms and Deviled Kidneys, and the vegetarian option of Swamp Sprouts with Blue Cheese Sauce.

"What do you fancy, Bertie?" Aldiss asked as his whiskers twitched in anticipation. Bertie, studying the blackboard carefully, simply shrugged.

"I can't choose," he replied. "It all sounds so good."

"Look," said Shona impatiently. "Why don't we go in, have a look around for Morag and Henry and, once we've found them, then we can decide what we're eating."

"Good plan, dear lady," said Bertie. "Follow me!"

Bertie pushed open the door into the restaurant, closely followed by the little brown rat and the rather concerned dragon. It was busy at breakfast, but there was no sign of Morag.

There were two groups of elderly witches sitting close to the fire, talking animatedly about the latest goings-on in their favorite supernatural soaps, particularly one featuring a magician called Christopholes, who was, in their words, "quite dishy."

In the corner, a huddle of wizards were discussing

whether or not someone had taken a dive during a recent football match, the consensus being that he had indeed and there was much muttering about the referee being "as blind as a bat." In front of each of them were plates piled high with food, and Aldiss and Bertie, whose stomachs were rumbling loudly with hunger, could not take their eyes off them.

Nearly all of the wizards had opted for "Eleanor's Human-Style Special"—a fry-up consisting of crispy bacon, eggs, potato scones, fried mushrooms, black pudding and baked beans. Only one of the witches, a fat lady with green hair, had opted for that; the rest had before them an assortment of different dishes including steaming hot green stews, scrambled egg and grilled frog or Eleanor's "Dieter's Special," spicy tadpoles on toast.

Seeing all that scrumptious fare, Bertie couldn't help himself. Forgetting momentarily about Morag, he sat down at the nearest table and took up the menu.

"Bertie!" Shona scolded. "This is no time to think about breakfast! We must find Morag and Henry! What could have happened to them since last night?"

"Oh yes, of course," he said. Suddenly he clutched his head and groaned as if someone had struck him. "Actually, now I come to think about it, I don't want breakfast. I don't feel well at all. In fact, I suddenly feel quite ill. I feel like I'm all battered and bruised and my head hurts." He put his head under his wing and moaned.

"Me too!" said Aldiss, leaping into a seat next to Bertie. "But I need a big strong cup of tea first. My mouth feels all dry and horrible."

"Hmm," said Shona, sitting down next to them. Her stomach was beginning to feel a bit cramped and she was definitely getting a headache. "Actually, I'm not feeling too good myself all of a sudden," she said. "This is all very strange."

"What is?" Bertie asked, his voice muffled from under his wing.

"Morag and Henry disappear and we all feel terrible the next morning. Do you think there's a connection?" Shona asked. She rubbed her belly thoughtfully.

"I don't know," replied Bertie. "But I wish this sudden pounding in my head would stop."

"What did we all have to eat last night?" Shona asked.

"I had the muesli, Morag had macaroni and cheese, Aldiss had . . . Aldiss, what did you have?" asked Bertie.

"Moon chicken stir-fry," said the rat, whiskers quivering. He winced at the memory. Although delicious last night, all of a sudden, moon chicken stir-fry did not seem so appetizing.

"And I had steak pie, broccoli, pickles and carrots," continued the dragon. "We didn't all have the same thing, so that doesn't explain feeling bad."

"Wait!" cried Aldiss. "Yes, we did. We all had cocoa just before we went to bed!"

"And none of us heard Morag and Henry leave during the night." Shona frowned. "Why do you suppose that was?" she asked. Aldiss and Bertie shrugged.

"Perhaps there was something in that cocoa that made us sleep soundly," she went on. "And if there was, we have to ask why someone would want to put us to sleep. I think something dreadful has happened to poor Morag and

Henry. They would never leave of their own accord, not without telling us where they were going."

"What do you suppose has happened to them?" asked Aldiss, his little eyes full of worry.

"You don't suppose that Henry was a spy after all, and he's handed Morag over to the Klapp demons?" ventured Bertie.

"I don't know," replied Shona. "But I think something amiss happened here last night and I aim to find out what." She got up. "I'm going to find that old woman. After all, she was the one who insisted we try the free cocoa."

❧

When they found the old woman, she was standing in the kitchen by the stove, stirring a large, black cauldron. She grinned when Shona began asking her questions.

"Where is the girl?" the dragon demanded. "And what have you done with her? What happened last night? Were we all drugged? Was it in the cocoa?"

The old woman said nothing, and continued to smile at the dragon. She had no intention of talking; she made that very clear, despite Shona's best efforts at diplomacy. The dragon, angered by the woman's determined silence, decided she would wait no longer for the answers she sought. Without warning, she grabbed the old woman by the throat and lifted her off the ground. Slowly, Shona began to shake her, her large claws wrapped tightly around her prisoner's neck, but not so tight that the old woman couldn't breathe.

"Tell me what I want to know, old woman, or I'll snap your neck in two!" warned the dragon, her nostrils flaring.

"I know nothing," gasped the woman pathetically. "Nothing, I swear."

Shona shook her again and tightened her grip around the woman's neck. Bertie flapped in horror and Aldiss jumped from foot to foot as the woman's face went bright red and then started to go purple. They urged Shona not to hurt her, but the dragon ignored them and squeezed a bit more.

"I . . . know . . . nothing!" the old woman gasped, struggling for breath. She pulled at the dragon's claws, but was not strong enough to loosen the grip.

"Granma Eleanor!"

Shona turned round to see a plain young woman in jeans and a frilly pink apron standing in the doorway. Her face was ashen with fear. She seemed rooted to the spot, but, then, without a thought for her own safety, the girl ran at the dragon and began to pummel her tough hide.

"Let go of my granma!" she pleaded. "Let go!" Her fists battered uselessly off Shona's side. The dragon barely flinched.

"Tell me where my friend is and I'll think about it!" she demanded. The old woman went limp in her grip.

"Oooh! Granma!" screamed the girl, terrified. "Let her go, please. She's 380, for goodness' sake! An elderly woman!"

"What has she done with the child?" said Shona.

The girl looked from the dragon to her grandmother and back again.

"I can't say," she said at last. "She'd kill me."

Shona gave the old woman's body a shake, causing her limbs to swing limply. The girl screamed.

"You better hope she gets to you before I do," the dragon said quietly.

"Okay, okay. I'll tell you. Granma sold her to MacAndrew. He was here last night on his way back to Murst. Granma had heard they were looking for more human slaves over there and thought the young girl you brought in would be perfect. She's still a little bit small, but they say if you get them young they're yours for life."

Bertie and Aldiss exchanged fearful glances.

"MacAndrew came during the night and lifted her out of her bed when you were still sleeping. Forget about her. He's taking her to Murst right now, so you've seen the last of her. That's it! That's all I know."

"But why didn't we hear anything?" said Bertie.

"Were we drugged?" asked Shona.

"Yes, yes. She drugged you. She put a sleeping potion in your cocoa. It was the only way she could get the girl off you." The granddaughter sobbed. "Now put my granma down, will you? She's too old to be going through this."

The dragon turned to Bertie and Aldiss, who both nodded to her to let go of the old woman. They were very relieved when Shona did as she was bid. However, Shona did not think about the old woman's comfort—there was no gentle lowering of her body. Instead, she abruptly unclenched her claws and let the elderly cook drop to the floor with a bump. The girl ran to her grandmother and, weeping, gathered her up into her arms.

"Oh, Granma, Granma," she cried. "Wake up, Granma, wake up! It's okay, the dragon has let you go."

As Shona, Bertie and Aldiss watched, first one then the other of the old woman's eyes opened. She blinked and then frowned.

"You sniveling, stupid fool!" she bellowed at her granddaughter. "You've told them everything! How many times have I told you to hold your tongue?"

"But—" whimpered the girl. "The dragon was killing you."

The old woman glared at Shona. "She wasn't," she spat. "I was pretending to be unconscious so she would think I was dead. And then you came along and ruined it."

She rose unsteadily to her feet. "And now you've gone and told them everything!"

"I'm sorry, Granma!" wailed the bewildered girl.

"You're going to be, you stupid girl! I suppose I'll just have to finish this myself! As usual!"

As the friends watched, the elderly witch—for a witch she was—turned to face them. Eyes on her tormentors, she fished a bottle of something green and hissing from her apron pocket, raised it high in the air and began to chant some ancient and terrible magic words. Shona looked in alarm at Bertie and Aldiss. She recognized some of those words and knew they were not good.

"Run!" she warned. "Hide!"

The dodo and rat ran for cover. Being small, it was easy for them to find hiding places in the cupboards of the kitchen, but it wasn't so easy for a dragon, even a pygmy dragon like Shona. She looked around frantically for somewhere to go, but it was all in vain.

The old woman cackled wickedly. Above her head, held tightly in her clawlike hands, the potion in the bottle began to swirl, and as she chanted, it bubbled and hissed even more.

Shona's eyes widened.

As soon as the potion threatened to boil over the neck of the bottle, the old woman sneered and threw it across the room at the dragon. For a split second Shona didn't know what to do; then her survival instincts kicked in. She saw something large and shiny—a large metal tray—close at hand. Quickly, she grabbed it and held it up it in front of her just as the bottle struck.

The explosion of sparks sent the dragon flying backward across the room, where she hit the wall and dropped to the floor. Before everything went black, she was sure she'd heard screaming.

❧

"Shona! Shona! Wake up!" There was a note of urgency in Bertie's voice.

"Please, wake up!" cried Aldiss. "We can't stay here, it's too dangerous!"

Shona's yellow eyes flickered open and she saw the concerned face of the dodo peering over her. Bertie immediately looked relieved.

"Oh, thank goodness," he said. "I thought you were done for. Come on, we must leave before anyone comes." Mustering all their strength, he and Aldiss took her arm and tried to pull her up.

She sat up and groaned. Her entire body hurt. She felt

like she'd been knocked over and flattened by a steam-roller. She rubbed her back and her head, but nothing helped.

"Ooooh, what happened?" she groaned. She got to her feet unsteadily and looked around to get her bearings. They were still in the kitchen of the restaurant. She looked to Bertie and Aldiss for an answer.

"Don't you remember?" asked Bertie, helping right her as she swayed unsteadily from side to side.

"No—I—what happened here?" she stared in aston-ishment, for all around her was destruction and disarray. The tables and shelves were scorched and blistered, and the walls were blackened with soot. Dishes and cups that had been sitting next to the sink to be washed now littered the floor in hundreds of smashed pieces, and the choking acrid smell of smoke hung low in the air.

On the floor lay the old witch, dead—her lifeless body blackened by the blast. Her granddaughter was lying at her side, unconscious and unmoving. Shona then remembered the potion being thrown at her; she remembered deflecting it with the large metal tray and being pushed off her feet by the force of the explosion.

"Did I do that?" she asked her friends. They both nodded.

"I saw it all happen," said Aldiss. "The bottle hit the tray and bounced back at the old witch. She tried to get away, but she was too slow. Her own evil potion hit her full force and killed her."

"What about her granddaughter?" asked Shona. She felt terrible that she had killed someone, albeit someone

121

who had drugged them all and sold their friend. Despite her earlier threats, Shona could never intentionally kill a living soul. "Is she dead too?"

"No, she's just unconscious," said Aldiss. "We've checked."

"Which is why we must leave now!" said Bertie urgently. "Before she comes round and calls for help. We must go."

Bertie picked up his satchel from the floor and he and Aldiss took Shona by the claw.

At first she was too shocked to move, but when Bertie gave her a tug, she pulled herself together and followed them out of the kitchen.

They hurried through the restaurant, startling diners in their wake, then out the doors and into the weak sunshine of the autumn morning. Bertie ruffled his feathers as the crisp cold air hit them, but he kept running with Aldiss scampering at his side and Shona bounding ahead.

"Whatever can we do now?" Aldiss gasped.

They both knew it was only a matter of time before someone called the Patrollers—Marnoch Mor's police force—and reported them. The three friends had to put as much distance between themselves and the lawpersons as possible . . . while there was still time.

❧

Morag thought she was still dreaming when she woke up and felt her bed tip. It rocked gently from side to side and would have been soothing had she not been aware that she hadn't lain in a cradle the night before.

She opened her eyes and looked around her. And this definitely wasn't the room she had fallen asleep in last night either. She sat up and winced. Ow! Her head hurt! She closed her eyes for a moment to let the pain pass and then opened them again. She was in a tiny whitewashed room with four little round portholes on the walls, beyond which were clouds. Then it struck her. She wasn't in a bedroom at all. She was in a cabin on a boat.

"So we're awake *now*!" said Henry sarcastically. "*Finally*, we're awake!"

"Morning," said Morag groggily.

"Morning! MORNING! Is that all you can say?" the medallion demanded. "After last night?"

"What happened last night?" She frowned. "And how did we get here?"

"I did everything I could to try and wake you," replied Henry, "but you slept right through the whole thing."

Morag was confused. She didn't remember a thing.

"I don't know what you mean," she said. "All I know is that I fell asleep in my bed in the room above the restaurant and now I appear to be in some sort of boat. What happened?"

The medallion sighed. "Shortly after you fell asleep, I was nodding off myself when I heard the bedroom door open. I couldn't see who it was until he came over and looked down at you. It was that ruffian from the restaurant."

"Hold on just a minute," interrupted Morag. "What ruffian?"

"The man who kept looking over at us in the restaurant, remember?" Henry said.

Morag did remember. "The hooded man?" she said. She hadn't liked him, and now look what had happened.

"Yes, he stole into your room in the dead of night. I tried to wake you by turning icy cold, but you were sound asleep. The hooded man crept over, pulled back the covers and lifted you out of bed. He grabbed your boots—they're under your bunk, by the way—and carried us out into the corridor."

"What did you do then?" Morag asked as she felt to see that the book her parents left her was still in her pocket. She was relieved to find it was.

"Nothing. What could I do? I couldn't fight him," said the medallion.

"But why didn't you use your magic?" asked Morag.

"There's a ban on using spells at Eleanor's due to the many and terrible fights that used to take place. Old Eleanor—she was in on your abduction, by the way—put a Cloaking Spell on the entire building.

"I could do nothing," he continued, a little regretfully. "All I could do was keep quiet in the hope that he hadn't heard me earlier. I figured that if he didn't know I was there, I could stay with you and hopefully help you later on.

"The hooded man quietly carried us downstairs, put us on the backseat of a car and drove off. We didn't go far. Then he stopped the car, took us outside and carried us down to a small jetty, where we were met by that giant woman he was talking to in the restaurant. This seems to be her boat. He paid her to take us somewhere, I couldn't catch what they were saying."

"And I slept the entire time?" said Morag.

"Like a log!"

"That's not right," she said, a little scared and confused. "I don't usually sleep like that. There must have been something in the food or something."

"I understand Eleanor drugged you," said the medallion.

"And what about the others? Where are they?" Morag wanted to know. "Do you think they're all right?"

"They're probably still sleeping in their beds," replied the medallion. "They would've been drugged as well, but they'll be fine."

But Morag wasn't so sure. Still, there was nothing she could do about it.

She had a proper look around her. She was in the belly of some sort of metal boat that smelled strongly of engine oil and fish. The engine chugged loudly somewhere behind her and the boat rocked gently from side to side as it cut its way through the waves.

There was nothing extraordinary about this cabin. The metal walls had been painted white some time ago, going by the look of it, as there was paint peeling in patches across the wall. Dots of rust rimmed the metal portholes with red, and a painted metal door in the wall was tight shut. There were two wooden bunks in the cabin, one that Morag had woken up in and the other against the opposite wall. Both were neatly made up with gray woolly blankets and crisp white sheets and pillowcases. The other was empty.

"Where are we?" Morag asked, bewildered. She peered out of the closest porthole, but her only view was that of the gray sea swelling against the side of the boat. She shivered at the sight of the freezing cold sea.

"It's hard to say, but the boat seems to be heading west," replied the medallion. "They didn't say when they left us here and I didn't ask. Didn't want them to know I could talk."

"Of course not," said Morag. She swung her legs off the bed and placed her feet on the floor. She still felt a little giddy and lightheaded, so she took her time to stand up. Her legs felt like jelly, and it took a couple of attempts to stand before she was finally on her feet.

She walked unsteadily to the door and tried the handle. It was locked. "Of course it is," she said, more to herself than to Henry. She walked back to the bunk and sat down. There was nothing else for it: she would have to stay put until whoever had kidnapped her decided it was time to come and get her. She pulled her knees up to her chin and closed her eyes. She was feeling very scared and very, very alone.

"Hoi!" said the medallion. "You're squashing me, you big lump!"

Morag looked down at the gold disc. He gave her a little smile and a wink and she smiled back weakly.

"Don't worry about a thing, dear girl," he said kindly. "I'll take care of you. Everything will be all right, you'll see."

"I hope so," replied Morag, tears pricking the back of her eyes as the boat rocked steadily onward.

10

It was seven o'clock in the morning and the sun was just peeping up at the horizon. The sky was in that hazy in-between stage, neither night nor day, not quite dark enough to be night and not quite light enough to be dawn.

The weather, too, hadn't quite decided what it was doing that morning. It was to be another cold day, there was no doubt about that, but the dark gray clouds still hadn't worked out when to offload their heavy cargo of rain. The wind, however, had made a decision that cold autumn morning; it was going to blow as hard as it could, and it was into this blustery day that Bertie, Aldiss and Shona ran.

After they left the restaurant, the three friends raced down to the harbor to seek out someone called Kyle the

Fisherman, a trusted human they had been told, whose family had a long history of ferrying magical folk. His fishing boat, called *Sea Kelpie*, was the only means to get them to the island of Murst.

The air smelled fresh and salty as they hurried down to the great stone walls that overlooked the harbor. There were about fifteen small fishing boats docked that morning, and there was not a single soul in sight.

Bertie looked in dismay at the boats bobbing gently in the dark gray sea. They all looked the same. They were all white with a blue trim. How were they going to find *Sea Kelpie* quickly? There was nothing else for it; they would have to read the names of every boat until they found the right one.

This made Bertie nervous because it was starting to get light and he didn't want to hang around and be seen by humans. That would be disastrous. He had heard of fellow Marnoch Mor residents leaving the safety of that magical place to venture into the world of men. They had never been heard of again, except one, a dwarf who had ended up as a clown in a circus. Bertie shivered at the thought, remembering how humans had treated dodos when they still lived together. There were very few of his kind left in Marnoch Mor, and none left in the human world. Mankind had seen to that. Dodos had been hunted to extinction. If he was seen, he'd be put in a cage and poked and prodded by scientists. Then he thought about Shona. If she was caught, there would be no telling what they would do to her. She would be put in a zoo or made to do tricks, or something equally horrible.

"Come on," Bertie said to the others. "Quickly. We can't get caught out in the open like this. Shona, you try over there. Aldiss, you look in the middle and I'll look here."

Without another word, Bertie began scanning the names of the boats. *Fancy Nancy, The Whistling Parrot, Orca's Dream, Annabelle* and *The Seven Seas*. No sign of *Sea Kelpie*. He went to help Aldiss, who was having trouble reading the names that had been rubbed out in places by the battering of the waves and the high winds. None of them were *Sea Kelpie*.

"Over here!" called Shona. "I've found it!"

Bertie and Aldiss ran over to her. The dragon was pointing excitedly to the bow of a little fishing boat tied to the end of a row of five others.

"There she is!" cried Shona. "The *Sea Kelpie*."

The dodo and rat looked and, sure enough, it *was* Kyle's boat. The question now was how were they going to get to it?

In an instant Shona took the lead. With a brave grin, she stepped gingerly onto the nearest boat and it rocked wildly. She kept her footing and moved on to the next one and the next and the next. All the little boats lurched under her weight, but she managed to jump onto the deck of Kyle's boat without falling overboard.

She waved for them to follow. First Bertie and then Aldiss leapt from boat to boat. The fishing vessels did not pitch as they had under Shona's weight; instead they just rocked gently, and within minutes the three friends were reunited on the deck of *Sea Kelpie*.

They found Kyle the Fisherman, fully dressed and curled up under a blanket on the top bunk of his cabin on board the fishing boat. He was unshaven and rough-looking, and was very obviously in a deep sleep. Bertie, who did not like the look of him, was not keen on waking him. He told his friends that he thought this was not a good idea, the man was obviously exhausted, and waking him would only cause problems. They would have to find someone else to take them. Then Aldiss argued that Kyle the Fisherman was the only human in these parts who knew about magical folk and was the only one who could take them to Murst, so they had to wake him. Shona agreed with Aldiss. Kyle snorted in his sleep and muttered something about singing a song. It was enough of a diversion to bring them all to their senses.

"Okay, we'll wake him," said Bertie uncertainly. He knew that time was precious and that there was little choice.

The fisherman slept heavily and it took them many attempts to shake him fully awake. He was a youngish creature and smelled of engine oil and tar. He was grumpy when they woke him and didn't appreciate being shaken awake by a large green dragon, a dodo and a rat. He sat up, yawned, rubbed his eyes and blinked hard.

There is a dragon on my boat, he thought. He sat up and looked at Shona fearfully. Although he had provided a service for magical folk for many years, he still wasn't completely used to dealing with them. He had never had to deal with a dragon before, and he most certainly was not keen on allowing one on board his fishing boat. That was just too much.

"Don't be alarmed," said Bertie. "We're friends and we need your help. We understand you know about Murst?"

"The DarkIsle?" he replied. Bertie looked at Shona. "That's what my father used to call it, anyway. He rarely mentioned it by name."

"Can you get us there?" piped up Aldiss.

"And if you can, how long would it take?" asked Bertie. "It's essential we leave immediately."

He shook his head sullenly. "Definitely not," he said. "Besides, no one knows where the DarkIsle is."

"Shona knows the way. We're on urgent Marnoch Mor business!" Bertie exclaimed with a pleading note in his voice.

If Kyle agreed to help them, Bertie went on, they would pay him handsomely. The fisherman started at the mention of money. He thought for a moment, then spoke.

"I'll take you and you," he said gruffly, pointing at Bertie and Aldiss. Then, looking at Shona, he added, "But I'm not taking that. I'm not having a dragon on board."

"What if we pay you double?" offered Bertie. He stuck a wing into his bag and began to rustle about for his wallet.

"No. Don't like dragons, and I won't have one on my boat," he said, shaking his head. "Now, if you don't mind, I'd like it to leave."

"Well!" said Shona, insulted and upset. She had never been called an "it" before. "I've never come across anyone as rude as you in my life. What's wrong with dragons? Why are you so against us?"

"Health and safety reasons," said the fisherman. "Fire regulations. You can't have a fire-breathing creature on board a boat, it's not safe."

"What if we told you she can't breathe fire?" said Bertie.

He gave Aldiss a shove as a warning. The little rat, who was the most truthful of creatures, had opened his mouth to say he was sure she did breathe fire, but thought better of it when he saw the warning look on Bertie's face.

"All dragons can breathe fire," replied Kyle. "It's what they do." He swung his feet off the bunk and leapt down to the deck. As he searched for his boots, the three friends tried to persuade him.

"Not me," lied Shona. "I'm of the breed that can't do it. I can't even fly. Look." And she turned round so he could see she didn't have any wings.

He nodded and Shona went on. "And look at me trying to breathe fire." She pretended to huff and puff and no smoke or sparks came out.

He nodded again.

"I'm perfectly safe," she tried to assure him. "I don't even bite." She grinned, showing two rows of perfectly vicious-looking teeth. Kyle recoiled in fright.

"And she's fully house-trained," offered Aldiss.

Shona shot the rat another look. "Yes, thank you, Aldiss," she said through gritted teeth. "I assure you, fisherman, that I will not cause you or your boat any danger. I only want to get to Murst." She looked at the man hopefully and gave him her most appealing look. "Will you allow me to stay on your boat? Please? It's very important."

The man thought for a moment and then shook his head again.

"No, I won't do it," he said as he pulled a boot on.

"But we need her," insisted Bertie, looking very worried. "It's getting lighter and it's essential we set sail as soon as possible. No one else knows the way to Murst."

"No, I'm sorry. I can't," replied the fisherman.

Shona frowned. "Well," she said. "You leave me no other choice!" She roared. The man backed away from her, eyes wide with fear.

"Wh-what are you going to do to me?" he stuttered. "What are you going to do to the boat?" He backed against a wall and could go no further.

Shona grinned. She licked her lips and stepped over so her face was directly in front of his. He recoiled from the rank smell of her dragon breath.

"Shona!" warned Bertie, who was scared she was going to do something rash.

"I," she bellowed to the shaking Kyle, "I am going to get your father!"

She smiled her fiendish dragon smile, which looked a bit gargoyle-ish, and turned to walk away from him.

"My father?" said Kyle, puzzled. "What do you want with my father?"

"Oh, don't worry. I'm not planning to eat him or

anything," she said. "I'm going to get him here and get *him* to take me to Murst," she added triumphantly. "Now, where's your phone?" She walked out of the cabin.

"You can't do that!" exclaimed Kyle. He followed her out. "You can't!"

"I can get your father to do anything I want," she replied, climbing up the stepladders to the bridge. "He owes me!"

"He owes you?" Now Kyle really was confused. How could his father owe a dragon anything? What had she done for him?

"Didn't your father tell you, when you were a little human," said Shona, "about a great storm that shipwrecked him on a strange dark isle off the west coast?"

Then Kyle remembered. His father had told him something. What was it again? His father had been in his boat far out at sea. The wind and the waves had picked up, the boat had capsized and his limp body had been washed up on the shore. He'd been close to death when he was found. The inhabitants of the island had nursed him back to health, and he was particularly fond of one of them. A girl called . . .

"Shona? *You're* Shona?" he asked in astonishment. "You're the one who saved my father's life?"

"The very one," she replied with a smile as she climbed up onto the bridge. It was quite small and her tail hung out of the door.

"Of course, it must be forty years ago. I was only a young dragonlet when I found him lying on the sand. At first, I thought he was dead, but I soon brought him round. Nice man, your dad," she said wistfully, then added, "Pity his son isn't more like him."

She hunted about for the radio, found it and tried to switch it on, but had no idea what she was doing. She looked at Kyle standing behind her, openmouthed and looking like he was trying to catch flies.

"I can't believe it," he said. "I always thought you were . . ."

"Human?" she suggested. "We made your father promise he wouldn't tell anyone about us. Could you imagine if he'd gone back to the mainland and told people there was a secret island out there beyond the horizon, with talking dragons living on it? He'd have been locked up, or if they had believed him, they'd have tried to find the island, to catch us or kill us or put us in their zoos. Now, how do you switch this on? I really would like to speak to Hector."

She flicked a few switches and the radio crackled a little, but remained resolutely silent. Kyle sighed and flicked the switches back to their original positions.

"You can't speak to Dad," he said softly.

"And why not?" asked Shona sharply. "*Why* can't I speak to him? I *demand* to speak to your father!"

"You'll have a hard time," replied Kyle. "He died four years ago."

Shona slumped back on her haunches. "Hector is dead?" she said. She had forgotten that humans didn't live as long as dragons. Tears brimmed in her big yellow eyes.

135

"I'm so sorry to hear that," she said, a teardrop running down her scaly face.

Kyle nodded in agreement and pulled an oily rag from his pocket for her to use as a handkerchief. The man and dragon shared a moment of remembrance before Bertie and Aldiss interrupted them. The dodo and rat had heard everything.

"Shona," said Bertie. "I'm sorry to be a nuisance, I know you've just been given sad news, but time is of the essence. If Kyle won't take us, we must find another way to get there."

Shona wiped a tear from her eye and sniffed. She got up.

"You're right," she said. "We must go." Without looking back at Kyle she strode out of the bridge and joined her friends on the deck.

"Wait!" Kyle called after her. "Wait! I'll take you!"

"You will?" cried Shona, delighted. "But I thought you wouldn't have a dragon on the boat!"

"That was before I found out you were house-trained!" He chuckled.

❦

On another boat far out to sea, Morag was hiding. She had heard loud heavy footsteps near her cabin door and, in a panic, had squeezed down the side of the bunk and pulled the covers over her head. Henry was very scathing about her choice of hiding place.

"Oh, they'll *never* find you in here!" he said sarcastically.

"Do you think so?" she asked, teeth chattering from fear.

"Of course they'll find you!" he snapped. "Silly girl. This is the first place they'll look!"

Clump, clump, clump. Silence. The footsteps stopped outside the cabin door. Morag pulled the covers tighter around her head and closed her eyes. She could hear someone jingling what sounded like a bunch of keys on a chain. A key went into a lock and turned with a loud scratching noise. The metal handle of the door was rattled and the door pushed open. It whined noisily. Clump, clump, clump. The footsteps came inside the cabin. She held her breath. Her heart beat loudly in her chest. It thumped so hard she felt it was going to leap out of her throat. She was shaking and clasped Henry tightly.

The footsteps moved closer and closer to where they were hiding. Closer and closer, and louder and louder. And then they stopped. The covers were grabbed from Morag's head and yanked away. Someone peered intently into her startled face.

"Ah, there you are!" said a very elderly giantess. "What are you doing down there?" she asked kindly. "Come on, up you get, on your feet."

She put out a hand for Morag and, not knowing what else to do, the girl took it. She hadn't expected the footsteps to belong to an old lady. She'd expected a big beefy man or a monster or she didn't know what, but not this. The tall old lady was surprisingly strong and swiftly pulled the shocked girl to her feet.

"Now, you sit down and I'll bring the tray in," she told

her. With a lazy wave of her hand, she indicated for Morag to sit on one of the bunks, but the girl was too stunned to move. The last few hours were beginning to get to her. She felt like she wanted to run away and hide and never come back, but of course she couldn't do that because she was now a prisoner on this boat.

"Sit down!" the old lady said again sharply. "Do as you're told, deary, and you and me will get on just fine. Don't do as you're told and you and me will have a falling-out, and we don't want that. Do you understand me?"

Morag nodded dumbly.

"Well, sit down, then, and I'll get you your tray."

Without taking her eyes off the old woman, Morag sat down on the nearest bunk. She suddenly felt very tired and very upset and wanted to cry, but she held back the tears.

The old lady clumped out of the cabin and came back seconds later with a huge tray bearing a steaming hot bowl of porridge, a plate of buttered toast, a glass of orange juice and a giant mug of hot milky tea. She put the tray on the bunk next to Morag.

"Now get this down you, you've got a long way to go yet," muttered the old lady as she turned her back to Morag and walked to the door.

"Wait!" said Morag. "Don't go yet. Where am I? What am I doing here?"

The old lady turned round and smiled.

"Don't you know, deary?" she said pleasantly. Morag

shook her head. "Ah well, that's not for me to say, then. You'll find out soon enough."

"But you're holding me prisoner against my will!" Morag cried. She stood up, and as she did so, her knee nudged the tray, sending the mug of tea rocking, spilling some of its hot contents. The old lady tutted, but did nothing to clean it up.

"Best get that down you before you lose any more," she chuckled.

"Where am I?" insisted Morag. "I demand to know."

" 'Demand,' is it?" the old lady said with a chuckle. "You'd best get rid of that attitude, deary. He doesn't like his maidservants having attitudes, you know. Of course, that all depends if he chooses you in the first place. He might not like you."

"Who won't like me? What are you talking about?" Morag wanted to know. The woman was talking in riddles.

The old lady looked at her as if she were weighing her up.

"Of course, there's no reason why he won't like you, you've got all the right attributes. Young, strong, pretty. You never know, when you're old enough you might be lucky enough to be chosen as his fourth wife. I hear he's looking for another," she said.

"Who is? Who are you talking about?" Morag took a step toward the old lady. She had intended to grab her and shake the information out of her, but the old lady was too quick. She stepped out of the cabin and slammed and locked the door before Morag realized what was happening.

"Eat up, deary," the old woman called from the other side of the cabin door. "We don't want you losing any more weight. You're skinny enough. He doesn't like them skinny, you know. You eat up and keep your strength up, you'll need it."

Cackling loudly to herself, the old lady walked away. Morag counted the footsteps as they walked along the corridor and went up the stairs.

"Oh, that was well played," said Henry. "You really got a lot of information out of her."

"Oh, be quiet, Henry!" said Morag crossly. She sat down on the bunk again and took up a piece of toast. Now she really was frightened. Who was this mysterious "he"? And, from what the old lady had said, was she to become a maidservant to this man? Or worse, his new wife?

Although she didn't know who she was going to or where she was being taken, Morag shuddered. For the first time in her life, she wished she were back at home with Jermy and Moira.

❧

High on the hill overlooking the harbor, two lanky, hairy creatures that stank very badly were watching the dragon, the rat and the dodo on the fishing boat. In their high-pitched voices, the creatures, Klapp demons, chattered to each other about what to do next. They knew that what they were witnessing—a dragon, a rat and a dodo getting on a fishing boat and probably heading for Murst—

might be important to their master, but, equally, they knew that when he went to Marnoch Mor on business, Devlish didn't like to be disturbed.

"I think we should tell him," said the larger Klapp demon, whose name was Tanktop (Klapp demons almost always had peculiar names—it was a tradition amongst their people to name their offspring after things from human catalogs. Tanktop had brothers and sisters called Skirt, Blouse, Stocking, Soft Leather Glove and Court Shoe). "Keep ourselves right. If this turns out to be really important and we don't tell him, he'll probably kill us."

"I'm not sure," said the other Klapp demon, whose name was Percolator. "Remember what happened to Kettle!"

They both shuddered. Kettle had been a rather small, particularly sneaky Klapp demon who had risen up through the ranks to become a general in Devlish's Klapp demon army.

One day, Kettle had discovered something he felt Devlish, who was away at the Witches', Warlocks' and Wizards' Convention in Marnoch Mor, should know. So, traveling under cars, he made his way to Marnoch Mor to his master.

On arrival, Devlish, who had been booed off stage at the convention, was in a stinking mood. He demanded to know why Kettle had disturbed him, and when the quaking demon gave him the information, he told Kettle it was irrelevant and turned him into a large bale of hay that was promptly eaten by the Shire horses tethered to Devlish's carriage (there are no cars in Marnoch Mor and everyone gets around by horse and cart or by walking).

"Nevertheless," said Tanktop, "I'm sure he might want to know about this. That boat is heading in the direction of Murst."

"We don't know that for certain," said Percolator.

Tanktop held a set of small binoculars up to his eyes. He nodded sagely.

"They're definitely heading for Murst," he said. "I can feel it in my bones. That dragon's going home, make no mistake about that."

"What shall we do?" asked Percolator.

"*We* are doing nothing," replied Tanktop. "*You* are going to go to Marnoch Mor to tell Devlish and *I* am going back to Murst. I want to see what that dragon, bird and rat are up to."

Percolator began to shake.

"Please, Tanktop, don't make me go tell Devlish. I don't want to end up being eaten by horses. Please, Tanktop," he pleaded. "I'll do anything else, but not that. He'll kill me."

Tanktop grinned, showing off a set of small, sharp and very yellow teeth. He put a long hairy arm around his Klapp demon comrade.

"Don't worry, Percolator," he said softly. "You won't feel a thing."

"Oooh, Tanktop!" the other demon sobbed. "Please don't send me. Please!"

Tanktop sighed.

"Just do it," he said. He lifted the binoculars again. "You must go and tell him. It's important."

"But—"

"That's an order!" barked Tanktop. He growled at his companion, baring his second pair of teeth, set, as they are with all Klapp demons, at the back of the mouth.

Percolator recoiled. He knew he had no choice. Tanktop was a senior officer in the Klapp demon Secret Police and he must do as he ordered. With a small sigh, he turned away from his superior and began to walk in the very ungainly, typically Klapp demonish manner down the hill.

"And hurry up!" shouted Tanktop after him. "Devlish needs to know about this immediately!"

Without turning back, the Klapp demon nodded and upped his pace. He began to run down the hill to the roadside where he would hide until a car or a truck went by. With a heart so heavy it felt like there was a large stone in it, Percolator reached the roadside and found a suitable hiding place. This is probably the last time I'll do this, he thought miserably, for Devlish will kill me as soon as look at me.

As he waited for a vehicle to pass, he deliberately did not look back up the hill to Tanktop. If he had, he would have seen Tanktop scuttle from his vantage point and run down the hill toward the harbor. There, Tanktop crept up to the row of fishing boats to which *Sea Kelpie* was tethered and made his way along the row of boats until he reached Kyle's. He boarded the little vessel silently and hid himself in a large vat used to store fish on trips out to sea. It was a perfect hiding place for a Klapp demon. No one would detect his kind's distinctive stench over the equally horrible smell of rotting fish.

11

Morag spent the entire day locked up in the cabin, her only companion the sarcastic and bad-tempered medallion. She occasionally saw the old lady, but only when she brought her food. Despite her pleas to learn more about her destination, the giantess would not tell her anything, and Morag became even more fearful about where she was being taken—and why. The hours passed as she lay on her bunk, her stomach churning with terror about what lay ahead. Eventually the droning hum of the engine and the gentle rocking of the boat encouraged her to drift off to sleep.

Morag slept without interruption. She hadn't realized how utterly exhausted she was, and despite the strangeness of the last few days and her fears, she didn't dream at all.

"Wake up, girl," a gruff voice said suddenly. "Come on, it's time to go."

She slowly opened her eyes. Standing before her, shifting from foot to foot, was a giant dark-haired boy dressed in armor. He wore a rusting metal helmet and held a battle-axe in one hand. He looked a little older than her, but was as tall as a grown human man and just as broad.

"Come," he mumbled. "You've got to get a move on. It's time to get off the boat. Mum says."

Morag sat up stiffly and yawned. Henry chinked quietly from underneath her pajamas. Without thinking, her hand went to her chest and she could feel the reassuring warmth of the gold medallion. At least she had one friend here, albeit a grumpy one. The giant boy did not notice her reaching for Henry and, instead, shyly threw her a large fur coat. It bounced off the sleepy girl and fell to the floor. He bent down to pick it up.

"Put this on," he said, offering the coat again. "You'll need it. And hurry up. My mother will be mad if you're not ready in time."

"Your mother is here?" Morag asked woozily. She had been sleeping too long in an awkward position, with her head bent at an angle, and it hurt. She swung her legs round and placed her feet on the floor.

"She's in charge," the boy said. "You've not met her yet, although you have met my grandmother. She was the one who brought you food."

He held the coat out to her again, and this time she took it. Slowly she got to her feet, pulled her boots on and heaved on the musty-smelling fur. It was large enough for a grown-up and felt heavy on her back. Its sleeves reached beyond her fingers and the hem trailed on the floor.

"Button it up," he said. "It's freezing outside."

Morag's fingers were stiff as she tried to press the large ivory buttons through the holes.

"Outside?" she said. "Are we leaving the boat?" Her heart leapt into her throat and she gulped. "Then we've arrived?" she ventured.

"We docked a few minutes ago," replied the boy. He looked at her anxiously. "Come on, hurry up, she'll be mad if I don't have you up on deck soon."

The boy waited until Morag fastened her coat, then pushed her gently out of the cabin. She blinked in the bright light of the corridor. The cabin had been more dully lit and this new light—from overhead strip lighting—stung her eyes. The boy gave her another nudge and nodded toward a flight of steep metal stairs. Wearily, she held on to the metal rails and began to climb. She felt dreadful—terrified and sick and lost and confused all at the same time. Her knees were weak as she climbed, and she gripped the cold rails for support, with the boy close behind, shoving her on.

"Where are we going?" she said, her voice wavy with dread.

"Up top," said the boy. "We've landed."

"Where have we landed?" she managed to ask before

her voice broke into nothing. She stopped in her tracks and looked round at the boy imploringly.

"Don't you know? Didn't Granny tell you?" he asked. He frowned, puzzled. "I thought you knew about this."

"About what?" Morag's voice came out as a squeak.

"Murst," he said. "We've come to Murst. You're to be sold to the daughter of the Great Warlock Devlish, up at Murst Castle. And Mum says we should get a good price for you. You look like you're used to hard work. Mum says . . ." He paused and looked up to the deck. "There she is!"

Taking a deep breath to calm her ragged nerves, Morag followed his gaze. Her eyes fell upon a huge woman in a tight-fitting purple velvet gown slashed to the hips. Underneath, she wore black moleskin trousers and black leather boots. She carried three swords on her belt. The woman had a mane of long black hair held back by a thick band of jewel-encrusted gold. She had one of the most striking faces Morag had ever seen. Although not beautiful, the woman was very attractive and there was a strong resemblance between her and her son.

Morag gasped. There was something familiar about her. Then she realized why—this was the woman who had been talking to the hooded man in Eleanor's restaurant. The woman smiled as Morag climbed up on deck. Morag did not return the smile.

"Fully rested?" she asked, and didn't wait for Morag to nod. "Good." She turned to her son. "Arrod, take the girl ashore."

"Yes, Mother." The boy prodded Morag gently in the back. "This way," he said, indicating the narrow gangplank. Morag slowly walked toward it.

"Arrod?" the woman called.

"Yes, Mother?"

"Hurry it up, we don't have all night. We've got to get rid of the produce and set sail on the next tide in two hours!"

"Yes, Mother." He grabbed Morag by the wrist and pulled her across the gangplank to a small wooden jetty lit up by fiercely burning wooden torches and lined by giant guards. The flames faltered in the sharp October wind and Morag shivered. Underneath the fur coat, she still felt chilled to the bone. She never once imagined things could get worse than life with Jermy and Moira and, now that they had, she felt very scared.

"Where are y-y-you t-t-t-taking me?" she asked her captor, her teeth chattering from a combination of fear and the cold. She pulled her wrist free from his grip and wrapped her arms round her torso in an attempt to hug some warmth into her body.

Arrod glanced down at her and looked away, as if ashamed of what he was doing.

"Up there," he said sternly, and pointed to the yawning gateway of a towering castle ablaze with the light of a hundred wooden torches stuck in rows up and down the gray granite walls. Ahead, giants in armor stood guard at the timber-gated entrance, on either side of which hung large red and gold banners that whipped angrily in the wind.

Morag could just make out the dark shadows of other giants marching slowly on the ramparts armed with enormous pikes. They marched steadily from one corner to the next and then, with a flourish, whipped around and marched back again. There were at least a hundred guards up there, Morag thought.

Light radiated from the numerous arched windows. Each pane of glass was made up of tiny kite-shaped pieces that glittered in the torchlight, like thousands of dancing glowworms. Every so often, Morag thought she saw someone walk by a window, but as soon as she looked more closely, the figure was gone, a fleeting silhouette in a castle full of shadows.

High above the fortifications, tearing up the passing clouds, were four enormous towers, one of which was bigger and grander than the others. Each displayed a large bloodred flag inlaid with gold, which flapped furiously in the wild weather.

Morag gasped. She had only seen such places in her history books at school and now here she was standing before one. If she hadn't had such a dreadful feeling about what was inside, she could have been excited.

She looked around desperately for some way to escape, but the jetty was lined with the giant guards and the only way onto the island was the steep narrow path up to the castle. A hooded man—the one from the restaurant—stood talking to a group of guards on the shore. He turned and winked at her as she passed by, but she ignored him, certain he had something to do with her present predicament.

Pushed on by the giant boy, Morag trudged up to the gate.

"Henry?" whispered Morag, barely moving her lips. "Henry, are you there?"

"Yes," he whispered back a little sleepily. "Have we arrived? I can't see anything."

"Yes," she hissed through her teeth. "Listen, I need your help. I have to get away from here. They're going to sell me," she said, hysteria rising in her throat.

"I can't do anything right now," he replied.

"But you're a magic medallion," she said. "Why can't you just magic me away from here?"

"My powers are limited," he replied mournfully. "I only do the basics—locating lost objects, psychic defense, precognition. I don't have the power to actually transport you, I'm afraid."

"But you said you could make whoever wore you invisible," she hissed.

"I embellished things a little bit to encourage you to let me come along," said the medallion. "You lot would never have let me come if you thought I could only do a few tricks here and there, would you?"

"Can't you at least do something that will stop this boy and let me make a run for it?"

"Run off into the wild woods of Murst? I don't think so, young lady," said the medallion. "It's too dangerous. There are wild bears and wolves and . . . other things in those woods, you know."

"Well, if you can't perform magic, maybe you could give me some advice instead?" she said in exasperation.

"Get inside the castle first, then appeal to the boy. He's your only hope."

"Him?" she asked aloud.

"What are you muttering about?" interrupted Arrod. "Wait. You're not doing a spell, are you?"

"No!" she replied lightly. "Just talking to myself."

She paused, thinking about how best to approach the boy.

"Arrod? That's your name, isn't it?" she began. The giant boy nodded. "Look, I really think there's been a mistake here," she went on. "I wouldn't make a good maid. I'm, I'm too lazy."

"Not my problem," said Arrod. "And anyway, it's my mum who wants to sell you."

"But *you* really don't want to do that, do you?" she said. "You're not the type who would sell another person into slavery, are you, Arrod? You seem so nice."

He stopped in his tracks and looked at her intently, as if he would uncover some deceit simply by staring at her. He must have been satisfied she was not trying to trick him, for he answered.

"Listen to me, girl," he began. "I *am* the type of person who would sell another. I've been doing it for years and I will continue to do it; it's what the family has done for centuries."

Morag nodded glumly. She fell into a moody silence.

"Try something else," urged Henry in a whisper.

"Did you hear that?" Arrod asked, his face awash with

152

puzzlement. "I could have sworn I just heard someone else speak."

Morag shook her head enthusiastically.

"Was it you?" he went on.

She shook her head again. "Maybe you heard the waves or the wind in the flags," she suggested. "It's funny what you think you hear when you're next to the sea."

"True," agreed Arrod. Then he said, "You sound like you know what you're talking about."

"I've lived next to the sea all my life," she replied.

"So have I!" He sounded interested. "I love the sea, me," he said. "One day I'm going to have my own trading ship, and then I'll make a fortune and I won't have to live with *her* anymore."

"Her?" asked Morag. Then it dawned on her. "Oh, you mean your mother!"

Arrod nodded. "She's a bit hard sometimes," he said a little sadly. "Not like mothers are supposed to be."

"And she makes you do *this*?"

"Do what? You mean sell slaves? It's the family business. It's expected."

"But you'd rather do something else?"

He nodded. "Yeah, I'd like to trade other things, like silks and diamonds and jewels and fine wines. Then nobody would get . . ." His voice trailed off and he looked at her.

"Hurt?" she suggested.

She stopped in her tracks. Maybe, just maybe, there was a chance for her to get free.

"Let me go, Arrod," she asked softly. "Tell them I gave you the slip. Please."

He looked back fearfully at his mother's ship. His mother was disembarking, striding confidently down the gangplank, barking orders to her crew. Then he looked at Morag, his great dark eyes full of regret.

"I can't," he said.

"Please." Morag wept. "I don't want to be a slave again. I was one before—I know what it's like. Please, Arrod, look into your heart and help me. You could hide me on your boat and let me off at the nearest port. There won't be any trouble. I promise."

He looked back toward his mother again. He sighed. His eyes closed for the briefest of moments and Morag held her breath.

"No!" he said finally. "Stop asking me to let you go. I can't, and that's that." He shoved her roughly. "Now hurry up, I don't have all night."

They said nothing else to each other until they got to Murst Castle's gate. They were waved in and the boy shut her in a little cell off to the left of the main gate. With a curt "good-bye," he locked the door and left her without looking back. In the pitch-darkness, she slumped to the ground and burst into tears.

"There, there," Henry said soothingly. "You did your best. Don't worry, we'll get out of here somehow. Just you leave it to your friend Henry."

"I can't leave it to you," she sobbed. "You've already said you don't have magical powers."

"True," said the medallion. "But I do have *some* powers, and we may get the opportunity to use them."

"What do you mean?" asked Morag as she wiped her tears on her furry sleeve.

"All in good time," the medallion said mysteriously.

12

In his hiding place aboard the little fishing boat, Tanktop the Klapp demon was feeling quite miserable. The boat had been sailing for hours and there was still no sign of it reaching land. He felt cold, cramped and hungry, but knew better than to come out until they hit land. He knew that if he was found, he would be tossed into the choppy sea and eaten by the fishes, so he stayed put in the lurching bowels of the boat.

Up on the bridge, Kyle was struggling with the boat's wheel and was beginning to regret agreeing to take them to Murst. The sea was getting wilder and the heavy sky was threatening to send a torrent of rain down on them. He pulled his sou'wester up tighter around his neck and stuck a battered blue cap on his head. The sea would not be kind to them today.

Down below, in the living quarters, Bertie and Aldiss were making plans about how they were going to find Morag and Henry and rescue the Eye of Lornish from Devlish. Shona, standing at the hatch, strained to hear what was being said over the whining of the boat's engines below.

"Hmm, it all sounds a bit risky to me," said Aldiss, shaking his head.

"Well, what else *can* we do?" snapped Bertie. He had come up with three plans so far and Aldiss had dismissed them all as "too risky."

"Wouldn't it be better," began Shona as she squeezed her great body a little bit more into the small cabin, "to wait until we get to Murst before we plan anything? Murst is a very rocky island. There's only one jetty for boats and that will be well guarded by Devlish's men. Unless we swim ashore, I can't see how we can land without being seen."

Bertie looked at her in dismay. All his plans involved landing elsewhere on the coast to allow them to sneak up to the castle and somehow find a way in to rescue Morag and Henry before they looked for the Eye. Now he would have to completely rethink it.

"Shona," he said, "tell me about Murst. You grew up there. What is the island like and where is the best place to land other than the jetty at Murst Castle?"

She frowned. She hadn't seen Murst since she had been turned to stone thirty years ago. She was sure it would have changed since then, but by how much?

"I can't think of anywhere safe for us to land other than the jetty," she said. "Unless . . . ," she muttered. Wasn't there another bay? she thought. She wracked her mind, trying to remember the coastline of the island.

Tapping her forehead with a big taloned claw, she fell silent with concentration. She tried to think back to her draghood—that's what dragons call their childhood. Wasn't there a place where she and her sisters used to play? Round at the north of the island? Was it far enough away from Murst Castle for them not to be seen?

"I think there might be a way," she said at last.

"Yes?" Bertie and Aldiss gasped excitedly.

"There's a place in the north," she said. "It would be too dangerous to land there. There's no jetty, no beach, only cliffs. But it's our only chance of getting on the island unseen. It's very risky and I'm not sure we should do it. We'd have to climb a sheer cliff-face, and *if* we made it to the top, there's ten miles to walk before we reach the Great Forest. Our problem there is it's full of dangerous creatures, and even if we could avoid them, we'd also have to be careful not to get lost.

"Before we get near the castle, we have to cross the great Murstlan River with its unpredictable currents and high tides. It would be exceedingly dangerous and I'm not sure we can do it."

"But it's our only way!" Bertie insisted. "We have no other choice!"

"Perhaps not!" Kyle the Fisherman called from behind Shona's great girth. The dragon looked round in surprise.

"What do you have in mind?" she asked.

"Let me squeeze by and I'll tell you," he said.

On the deck, Tanktop, still feeling seasick, crawled out

of his hiding place. He got as near as he dared to the cabin and listened intently at an open porthole.

Inside, Bertie nodded as Kyle spoke. The human's plan was quite clever, the dodo thought. It was simple and not without risks, but at least they wouldn't be swimming through turbulent waters, scaling any treacherous cliffs or defending themselves against dangerous animals. When Kyle finished, Bertie turned to Aldiss and Shona.

"Well? What do you think?"

The rat and dragon looked serious, then Aldiss spoke.

"I think it might just work," he said.

"So do I," said Bertie. "Shona?"

The dragon nodded. "I'm in," she replied.

Bertie smiled. "That's agreed, then. Let's all get some rest. We've still got a fair bit to go, and we won't get to Murst before nightfall. Now, I don't know about anyone else, but I am very hungry. What would you all like to eat?" he asked.

Kyle looked perturbed.

"I don't have much for eating on this boat," he said hurriedly. "But if you give me a couple of hours, I'm sure I can catch some fish."

"Oh, don't worry about that." Bertie smiled, and patted his satchel. "I can soon rustle up anything you want. Just ask."

The fisherman looked at him dubiously. "And how might you do that?"

"With this," Bertie replied, holding up the bag. "Go on. Anything you want. Just ask."

Kyle frowned. He could ask for any dish he wanted and

he couldn't think of one. Then a memory popped into his head, a memory of when he was a boy and his father used to make him the one meal he truly loved.

"Okay," he said. "Ask it to bring me a plate of my dad's mince, mashed tatties and beans."

"No problem," said Bertie. He placed a wing inside the bag and pulled out a large plateful of the most delicious-smelling, piping hot minced beef, mashed potatoes and baked beans. Kyle stared at it in amazement as it was placed before him.

"Aldiss," continued Bertie. "Any requests?"

Above them, the very hungry Klapp demon was licking his lips. He was being driven to distraction with the delectable smells steaming through the open porthole. The rat, he saw, had chosen a cheese and onion omelette, one of Tanktop's favorite meals, and the dragon had opted for roast chicken, potatoes and carrots. The dodo who was handing out the food had decided on a vegetarian curry with rice.

Tanktop could hardly contain himself. The aromas coming from the cabin were heavenly. He decided to risk having a look. The creatures inside would be too busy eating to spot him, he told himself. He just had to see the wondrous oven that was creating all this mouthwateringly lovely food. He cautiously peeked over the edge of a porthole into the cabin. The human, the dodo and the rat were eating at a little table. The dragon was in the doorway, wolfing down her chicken. Tanktop looked around and couldn't see anything that could have produced these meals so quickly, and he wondered what had brought all this food to the boat.

"Drinks, anyone?" he heard Bertie ask.

He watched the dodo put his wing in his satchel and take out a glass of milk for the dragon, two glasses of cold beer for the human, a small cup of hot chocolate for the rat and a cup of tea for himself. "All courtesy of the bag!" The dodo laughed.

"The bag!" muttered the Klapp demon to himself. *"It has powers."*

He stole away from the window and crouched in his hiding place, the wonderful smell of food following him. His stomach rumbled as he thought of that moist chicken and delicious mince and the cheese and onion omelette and the curry.

"I deserve it more than them," he whispered to himself. "And I'll have it!"

A plan began to hatch in his ugly hairy head. If he could steal that bag, he could eat whenever he wanted and would never go hungry again. Stuff Devlish, he thought. He would live like a king and never have to spy on anyone again—but only if he could steal the bag.

13

Tanktop waited until there was quiet on the boat before venturing from his hiding place again. The wind and rain had abated and the sun was making weak attempts to come out from behind the clouds. It wasn't as cold as it had been, but he shivered as he tiptoed his way across the deck. The dragon had left the cabin and was talking to the fisherman up on the bridge. Both had their backs to the Klapp demon, so they didn't notice the stinking creature make his way back to the porthole.

"Two are away, so that leaves two," the hairy creature muttered as he positioned himself outside the cabin. "The two little ones . . . hmm, this should be easier than I thought!"

He put his long monkey-like hands up to the porthole to steady himself and peered in. The cabin was silent save for a snoring Bertie lying propped up on cushions on a bench at the little table. The rat lay curled up underneath, his little body gently rising and falling as he breathed.

The Klapp demon looked around the cabin. He spotted the satchel lying at Bertie's side under the tips of his outstretched wing. The bird was relaxed against it, but Tanktop still thought he would not wake if he—the best Klapp pickpocket and thief of his clan—were to ease it out from under him.

He came away from the porthole and peered nervously up at the bridge. The dragon and the man were still deep in conversation. So quietly, with the stealth of a cat, Tanktop made his way to the cabin doorway and carefully pulled the door open. The rat and the dodo were still asleep inside, oblivious to the master thief creeping in on them. He silently took a couple of steps down the little ladder into the cabin, and closed the door behind him so that he couldn't be seen from the bridge. Toenails quietly clicking on the wooden steps, he slowly made his way inside.

Aldiss, who was dreaming of cheese, was the first to notice the unmistakable acrid smell of Klapp demon. But the little rat thought he was still dreaming and moved to protect his imaginary cheese. His little nose twitched as the hairy creature crept closer, but the stench was not enough to wake him.

Bertie, who had never had a great sense of smell, stirred in his sleep. He was dreaming about maps and jetties and cliffs when suddenly something strange happened. A map of the island turned black and started to burn, and the choking smoke made him drop it on his claw, causing him to squawk. He whimpered and his tail feathers trembled in his sleep. Tanktop froze. He stared at the bird until it stopped moving again and carefully reached across. Sliding his fingers under Bertie's protective wing, Tanktop took hold of the corner of the satchel.

Slowly, slowly, gets the bag, Tanktop thought as he loosened it free from Bertie's grasp. The Klapp demon licked his lips. He was already thinking about the delicious morsels he was going to pull from it: pork rinds and offal, chicken fat and kipper heads, and his favorite meal of pig's trotters, cold congealed peas and overcooked sprouts. Saliva dripped from his lips and pooled on the table with a soft splosh. The sound caused Aldiss's ears to twitch.

"Bertie, that you?" the little rat murmured in his sleep, eyes still closed, head tucked in tight.

Bertie did not answer. Tanktop held his breath. Aldiss fell silent again. Tanktop sighed with relief and, clutching the bag to his hairy chest, quietly backed out of the cabin.

He tiptoed to the bottom of the stairs. A quick look around assured him that all was quiet, and he began his slow ascent to the deck. Silently congratulating himself on his clever theft, the Klapp demon stealthily opened the cabin door. There was no noise as the door swung open and . . .

Tanktop shrieked and his heart leapt into his mouth. Lunging in before him were the dripping, snarling teeth of an incensed dragon. With nostrils flared and yellow eyes burning, Shona growled low and deep, ruffling the Klapp demon's wiry hair. Tanktop gasped, his eyes rolled and he fell backward in a faint. His body dropped noisily down the stairs and he landed with a grunt in the cabin below. The bag bounced after him and landed nearby.

Woken by the commotion, Bertie and Aldiss leapt to their feet in fright.

"What? What?" spluttered Aldiss incredulously. "What's a Klapp demon doing on board this boat?"

"It was making off with your bag, Bertie," called Shona from the deck. "Until I smelled his putrid stench."

Tanktop was still groaning. The fall had woken him out of his faint and now he looked up at two furious animals, a dodo and a rat, standing over him. He sat up and rubbed his back and looked at them fearfully.

"Well?" said Bertie. "What do you have to say for yourself, demon?"

Tanktop swallowed hard. "A thousand apologies for the disturbance—*Your Majesty*," he tried lightly. He started hacking and his normal growling voice returned. "I was only protecting your bag for you in case some beast like this evil, lying dragon lady should creep in and steal it . . . Your Majesty." Tanktop tried to look innocent.

Bertie was not deceived.

"First of all, kindly stop calling me 'Your Majesty'; I am not royal nor ever likely to be," he snapped. "Secondly, kindly stop lying to us. It's clear what you were doing. Tell the truth or . . ." Bertie looked around him for inspiration—for something to threaten the Klapp demon with. "Or I'll feed you to *her*."

Shona, who was looking down from the deck, made a nasty face on hearing this, but quickly changed it to a snarling one when Tanktop looked up at her to see if Bertie meant what he said. She licked her lips as if he were the tastiest thing she had ever seen and the Klapp demon shrieked again in fright.

"Please, I don't want to be dragon feed, sir, I'll tell you the truth," he whimpered. "I was only going to borrow the bag, Your Honor, not steal it. I wanted something to eat. I'm so hungry, my lord! I could eat my own hands. Look!" And the Klapp demon pretended to munch on one of his fingers. "And just listen to my stomach rumbling. Take pity on me, sir, please. I am *so* hungry."

Bertie looked at the pathetic creature before him and sighed. He snatched up his magic satchel and held it close to his feathery breast. Patting it lovingly, he checked it for any obvious signs of tampering or damage. Happy his bag was still in one piece, he slung it over his shoulder and silently vowed never to let it out of his sight again. He turned to the Klapp demon, still cowering before him.

"What would you like?" Bertie asked. He was trying to be kind, but his voice sounded a little angry.

The Klapp demon looked at him suspiciously.

"Sorry, sire, I don't know what you mean. I'd like a lot of things, you see. Can you be more specific?" Tanktop said. His mean little eyes darted from Bertie to Aldiss and then to the dragon. They were all watching him intently.

"What would you like to eat?" Bertie asked in exasperation. He really couldn't be bothered with this stinking, horrible creature, but he had a kind heart and he couldn't see a fellow creature starve. "Hurry up, I don't have all day."

Tanktop thought for a moment and then answered: "A pot of boiled fish eyes and some raw carrots," he said.

"Well . . . eh . . . er, I'll see what I have. What is your name, creature?"

"Tanktop, sir. I was named after my grandfather," Tanktop replied proudly.

"Well, er, Tanktop. If you want a pot of boiled fish eyes and some raw carrots, you shall have it," said Bertie. Shona and Aldiss gasped. They couldn't understand why Bertie was being so nice to this disgusting Klapp demon.

Tanktop rubbed his great hairy hands together and bowed. "Why, thank you, sir. You are a most kind sir."

Bertie held up a wing. "I haven't finished yet," he said. "If you want the food, first you must do something for us."

"Anything, sir, anything," replied the Klapp demon, licking his slavering lips. Oooh, I'd do anything for a pot of boiled fish eyes and raw carrots, he thought.

"First you must tell us what you're doing here and what you know of Devlish."

Except that! Tanktop, who had been staring greedily at the bag, looked up at Bertie with real terror in his eyes. He didn't mind admitting to these animals what he was doing on the fishing boat, but he couldn't, just couldn't, speak about his master. It was out of the question. What if

Devlish found out? His spies were everywhere. He would find out that he, Tanktop, was telling these enemies about him, and then Tanktop would be as good as dead. The Klapp demon whimpered and sat down dejectedly on the floor of the cabin. He would not eat tonight because he would not tell them anything about his master.

"Well?" the dragon roared from above. "We're waiting."

Tanktop curled himself up into a tight ball of matted fur and began to wail. At first the wailing was soft, but very soon it rose into a loud noise.

"Don't make me tell," he cried. "Please don't ask me any questions about *him*. It's not fair. I can't tell you anything! I don't know anything! Please don't make me!" He tucked his head under a lanky arm and refused to come out.

Bertie knew how to entice him. He put his wing into his bag and pulled out the bowl of steaming hot boiled fish eyes. He passed the bowl to Aldiss who held it out, as far away from the Klapp demon's nose as possible. The smell wafted around the little cabin and played havoc with Tanktop's nostrils. He stuck his head out for a look and his eyes fell on the bowl.

He put out his hand. Aldiss drew back the bowl.

"Well," said Tanktop, uncurling himself. "I suppose it would be okay to tell you a little of why I'm here," he said, saliva dripping from his sharp little teeth. "We were on a scouting trip when we saw you," he began. He sniffed deeply. The smell was intoxicating.

"We?" repeated Bertie.

The Klapp demon saw his mistake. "Did I say 'we'? I meant 'I.' *I* was on a scouting trip and *I* saw you, so I thought you must be up to something, so I followed you. I didn't know you would be taking a long trip somewhere across the seas, above the dangerous fishes. I didn't. Honest!"

"Why were you interested in us?" Aldiss wanted to know.

The Klapp demon looked maliciously at the little rat. He was desperate for something to eat, and this vermin was in the way.

"Well?" asked Bertie. "Answer his question."

"You looked suspicious. I could see you were heading for Murst. My master would reward me if I found out what you were doing. Give me the bowl, please, sire." The Klapp demon lunged for the bowl, but Aldiss whipped it out of his reach.

"Who knows you're here?" Bertie asked.

"No one, sire, not anyone, not Devlish, not no one," replied the hungry creature. "Give Tanktop the food, sire. Give me the food," he pleaded. His eyes never left the bowl of fish eyes. "I haven't eaten for days."

"So Devlish knows we're here, then?" Shona called from the top of the stairs.

Tanktop turned to look up at her. He put on his best innocent face and groveled.

"Oh, dear dragon lady, no," he cringed. "No one knows Tanktop is here." That, at least, was the truth.

There was a silence as the three friends took in what the

demon had said. None of them trusted it. After a pause, Shona spoke.

"Give him the food," she said. "Then you and Bertie come up to the deck and we'll decide what to do with him."

Aldiss put the bowl down in front of the Klapp demon and climbed the stairs after Shona and Bertie. As soon as the bowl had been laid at his feet, Tanktop pounced and brought it up to his lips. Fish eyes spilled out either side of his greedy mouth as he slurped the food down. Stupid animals, he thought. I am too clever for you.

Up on deck the three friends convened to talk.

"He's lying," said Bertie.

"No doubt about that," said Aldiss.

"What shall we do with him?" asked Bertie.

"Let me chomp him in two and we can throw the body into the sea," suggested Shona. The other two looked at her in horror. "What's wrong with that?" she asked innocently. "That's what they used to do with demons in the old days. Don't tell me you want to keep him as a pet?"

"We can't kill him," said Aldiss. "That wouldn't be right."

"We can't let him go either," replied Shona.

"Shona's right," Bertie said. "He would go straight to Devlish and warn him we were on our way. That is, if whoever was with him hasn't told Devlish already. He was definitely lying about being on his own. No, we should keep him locked up here. Once we've found Morag and rescued the Eye we can take him back to Marnoch Mor and let Montgomery deal with him."

He added, "Besides, the demon must have been inside Murst Castle, so he may be useful to us. Aldiss, lock the door to the cabin. Shona, check all the portholes and make sure they are closed tight. We can't afford to let this Klapp demon out, not just now at any rate."

With the Klapp demon safely locked away in the cabin, Bertie and Aldiss joined Kyle on the bridge. Shona sat outside on deck, shivering in the biting wind and cold spray that washed over the boat every now and again.

"How much longer till Murst?" Bertie asked Kyle, handing the man a steaming hot mug of tea from his satchel.

"I reckon we'll get there by tomorrow morning. Isn't that right, Shona?" he called to the dragon.

Shona, who had found a tarpaulin and was pulling it over her body, nodded glumly. "Murst is still some distance away, and it feels like it's going to be another cold night." She shivered.

"Best bunk down in here for the night," said Kyle to the others after they had told him about capturing the Klapp demon. "There are some blankets in that box behind you."

"What about you?" asked Aldiss.

"I'll be all right," said Kyle. "I'm used to being up all night fishing."

"Come on, Aldiss," Bertie said, lifting the lid of the box. "Give me a hand with these blankets, will you? It's going to be a long night."

"Do you know any sea shanties?" the rat asked Kyle, causing the big burly fisherman to laugh.

"Know any?" he said with mock horror. "My family wrote most of them."

And with that he burst into a song about sailors and mermaids and far-off lands and before long, the exhausted rat and dodo were curled up under the warm blankets, fast asleep, as the *Sea Kelpie* rocked onward.

14

Morag was in the castle's cramped dark cell for what seemed like an age before the door opened and torchlight flooded in. A small dark figure stood silhouetted in the doorway.

"Come," the figure said. It was a woman. "It's time you joined the rest of us." The voice was flat, matter-of-fact, and not at all kind.

"I'm not going anywhere with you," said Morag defiantly. "Let me go. You can't make me go with you and be a servant and that's that."

"You tell her!" whispered Henry.

The woman at the door sighed as though she had heard all this before.

"Get up off your backside and follow me!" she snarled. "I'm not taking any insolence from someone like you. You're here now and you've been chosen to be my lady's maid, and that is quite an honor. So whatever is bothering you, get over it. Now get to your feet!"

Stung by her harsh words, Morag scrambled to her feet. She recognized that tone of voice right away. It sounded like when Jermy and Moira were angry. Morag knew better than to go against this woman's wishes. She had the kind of voice that belonged to someone who might beat her and she didn't want to make her any angrier.

"Make it quicker next time," said the woman, voice flat and calm again. "Now come over here."

Morag meekly walked to the door. The woman put out her arm as if she was going to cuddle her. Instead, she struck her over the back of the head.

"Ow!" Morag squealed in pain.

"That's for not coming right away," said the woman. "Disobey me again and you'll be whipped, girl, do you hear me?"

Morag didn't answer. She just rubbed her aching head.

"I said, do you hear me?"

"Yes," she whispered, tears of fear stinging her eyes.

"Yes, Madam Lewis," said the woman.

"Yes, Madam Lewis," repeated Morag.

"Good," she replied. "Now come with me. You've got a lot to do before you can sleep tonight."

In her oversized fur coat, Morag followed her out into the courtyard. The flickering flames of the wall-mounted torches cast long shadows over the guards, making them look even more sinister. She kept her head down and did not look at them, but could feel their curious eyes on her.

The courtyard was sheltered from the worst of the winds, but that did not stop the rain from falling. Even though she had her boots on, Morag still managed to slip and slide on the wet cobbles as she hurried across the square to keep up with the quick marching strides of the formidable woman.

It was only as she followed the bobbing figure of Madam Lewis that Morag realized the woman was different from the other people she had seen within the castle. She was no giant, but was thin and bony and only a few inches taller than Morag herself. She wore a long dark gown and ankle boots with a short heel. Her dark hair was dragged back from her face in a severe top knot. Her flaming red cheeks made her look like the Judy doll from a Punch and Judy booth, Morag thought. She had nasty, mean eyes like Mr. Punch too, to match her nasty, mean temper.

She took Morag up to a pair of massive wooden doors that were yanked open by giant guards, who bowed to Madam Lewis as she stepped inside, their great bulky bodies dwarfing her and the girl. Madam Lewis ignored them and swept past with Morag hurrying behind.

They entered a large dimly lit hallway decorated with ferocious-looking swords and broad shields, and scores of macabre hunting trophies. The mounted heads of deer, elephants, lions and bears looked dolefully down on them as they walked past. Large tapestries of hunting scenes hung from the ceiling to the floor, and as she walked past, Morag noticed the tapestry archers were chasing dragons, birds and small creatures. In other scenes men and women and children clung on to one another against the approach of lightning, and just before the tapestry ran out, she saw that the last scene showed a woman standing in a room surrounded by paintings of despairing faces.

The hallway ended in a broad flight of stairs with an ornately carved wooden banister. On one wall, a small dying fire gave out the last gasps of flames in a stone fireplace big enough to walk into. Opposite it was a locked door, as large as the one they had entered.

Morag had never seen anything quite so awe-inspiring before. She slowed her pace to look around.

"Come with me," snapped Madam Lewis. "And don't dawdle." She hurried to a small door under the stairs. Without saying a word to Morag, she opened it and slipped inside. Morag hesitated. "I *said*, don't dawdle, girl," the woman growled from within. Morag followed her inside.

The little door led to a narrow stone stairwell that wound its way downstairs. Although dry, the stone stairs had been worn smooth by centuries of use, causing Morag to sometimes slip as she hurried after Madam Lewis. Eventually, they came to a landing and Morag watched as another door was opened.

Behind this door was a warm room, where a fire provided the only light to see by. Compared to what she had seen of the rest of the castle, Morag thought it looked quite small and cozy. In the center was a long wooden table surrounded by many chairs, three of which, Morag was surprised to see, were occupied by a man and two women. More humans, she thought. On the table was a white teapot and three large mugs.

"Follow me, hurry up," snapped Madam Lewis as she walked by the table, barely glancing at the people seated there. They, in turn, ignored her, but stared at Morag as she hurried by. She felt the color rise in her cheeks, and put her head down and did not look at them. Madam Lewis led her into yet another small room and stopped. She opened a chest sitting against the wall and started to pull out some clothes.

"This," she said, handing Morag a gray dress and a brilliant white apron, "is your uniform. And this," she continued, placing a set of red pajamas in her arms, "is your night attire. And these," she added, giving Morag a pair of sensible black shoes, "are for your feet." She looked disdainfully at Morag's green boots. "They should fit you all right."

Morag looked at the pile of clothes in her arms and nodded glumly.

"Now, follow me." She walked through a door at the far end of the room that led out onto a landing and yet another staircase. Morag saw that it wound up and up and up, out of sight. They passed several landings and doorways, but still Madam Lewis climbed higher and higher.

Eventually the staircase ran out of stairs and they reached the very top where there was a small wooden door that led into a large dark room. This, Madam Lewis informed Morag, was where she was to sleep. In the dim light cast by a small lantern, Morag could make out four beds, three of which were occupied by other girls.

"You can sleep over there." With a long bony finger she motioned toward the empty bed in the corner. "And I'll see you in the morning."

With that, she turned and left the room. Morag listened to her footsteps as they descended the stairs outside. She sighed and looked around the dim room, thinking miserably of her fate. She wished again that she was still living with Jermy and Moira. At least she knew where she was with them.

One of the girls was snoring loudly in the corner and the other two looked like they were asleep. No time for introductions tonight, thought Morag, her heart so sad and heavy it felt like it was full of lead. She took her bundle of clothes over to the bed and placed it on the floor. Carefully, she took off her boots and placed them neatly beside the clothes. Next off was the fur coat. She took out her parents' book, and slipped it under the pillow and climbed under the heavy covers of the bed. Holding Henry tightly in her hand, she fell fast asleep.

Morag felt she had barely closed her eyes when she was roughly awakened by someone shaking her.

"Get up, get up!" said a voice. "It's time to get up!"

She opened her eyes and blearily looked to see who was talking. A girl who looked a couple of years older than

Morag was standing by her bed. Her fair hair was neatly tied back in a ponytail and she was wearing a similar uniform to that which Morag had been handed the night before.

"Come on or you'll be late!" urged the girl, grabbing Morag by the arms and pulling her.

Still groggy with sleep, Morag slowly sat up. Forgetting about Henry, she stretched her arms up high above her head and in doing so, exposed the gold medallion to the girl, whose eyes lit up.

"Oooh, what's that?" she asked, reaching for it. Morag hastily tucked him out of sight under her shirt.

"Nothing," she said.

"That don't look like nothing," said the girl. "Let's see it!"

Morag held Henry protectively to her chest. For some reason, she didn't feel she could trust this girl and she didn't want her looking at the medallion.

"Come on, let's see it!" she said, greedy eyes never leaving Morag's hands.

"No," said Morag firmly. "It's not worth looking at."

The girl scrutinized Morag, then shrugged and smiled. "Never mind," she said. "I'll get a look at it some other time." She smiled again. "Now come on, you've got to get up, otherwise old Lewis will do her nut."

The girl told Morag her name was Chelsea and instructed her to get dressed quickly. It was cold in the small attic bedroom, and Morag shivered as she removed her sweater and pajamas. They were to meet Madam Lewis down in the kitchen in ten minutes sharp, Chelsea told her as she helped her on with her dress. Morag slipped her book into one of the side pockets.

"We'll have breakfast and then we'll get our instructions for the day," she said.

Breakfast sounded like a great idea to Morag, whose stomach was already rumbling loudly, and she wondered what it would be. A big plate of bacon and eggs would be great, she thought a little more cheerfully. She pulled on her shoes, which were slightly too big, tied the laces and then waited for Chelsea to show her the way. The girl hesitated again.

"Show me the gold thing," she demanded. "I want to see it."

"No," said Morag. "It's nothing."

"If it's nothing, then show it to me."

"I said no," said Morag firmly. She was determined not to let this girl bully her.

Chelsea grinned and made a grab for the medallion. With a shriek Morag slapped her hand out of the way. But that did not stop Chelsea. She went for the medallion again, this time knocking Morag to the ground and grabbing at Henry. Morag held her off, kicking her shins and pushing her grasping hands away. The two rolled around on the floor, shrieking and clawing and biting and kicking.

"GIRLS!"

The shock of the exclamation broke the two apart and they lay on the floor gasping for breath. Madam Lewis, her face the picture of fury, was standing in the doorway, tapping a birch cane off her left hand. She moved toward them, eyes like slits. Chelsea sat up and tried to appeal to the woman.

"I'm sorry, Madam Lewis, I'm sorry. She started it, honest!" she cried, but her pleas fell on deaf ears.

Madam Lewis lifted the birch cane above her head, and brought it down with a swoosh, hard on Chelsea's shoulder. The girl squealed in pain as Morag watched, horrified. Then she turned on Morag, who had curled up into a ball, as tight as she could. She held her breath and waited for the pain of the cane's hard whack, but no pain came.

Unable to work out what had happened, Morag peeked up at Madam Lewis. The woman was standing stock-still, cane stiff in the air, an expression of fury fixed on her face. At her feet, Chelsea was still cowering, but was also not moving. Morag uncurled and sat up and looked at the pair in astonishment.

"What's happened?" she said out loud.

"I wasn't going to let her hurt you," said a voice from under her clothes. "So I froze them."

"You froze them, Henry?" Morag repeated. She scrambled to her feet and went to look more closely at Madam Lewis. Waving her hand in front of Madam Lewis's face, she could not make the woman blink or flinch. "She's not dead, is she?" she asked.

"Unfortunately not," he replied. "But she won't know what's happened. Uh-oh. Watch out, she's coming out of it."

Morag stood back and watched as Madam Lewis and

Chelsea slowly thawed out and came back to life. Madam Lewis looked perplexed as she lowered the cane and Chelsea was confused. They said nothing as they slowly regained their senses. Morag stayed quiet. Madam Lewis sighed and looked around the room like she had never seen it before.

"What was I saying?" she asked, looking directly at Morag.

"That we had to go down for breakfast and then you would give us our instructions for the day," she replied quickly.

"Very good," Madam Lewis said. Then she saw the girl at her feet. "Chelsea!" she said sharply. "Get up off the floor, girl. What on earth do you think you're doing down there?"

"I don't know, Madam Lewis," replied Chelsea, as she rose.

"And tidy yourself up," said Madam Lewis harshly. "You look a state."

Chelsea hastily fixed her disheveled clothes and retied her hair into a ponytail. Morag, too, smoothed down the apron of her uniform. Madam Lewis studied both of them carefully as if she were looking for flaws, looked satisfied and led the way to the door.

"Right," she said. "Follow me."

Chelsea trotted behind her quickly and Morag followed. As she entered the stairwell, she whispered quickly to Henry.

"How did you do that?"

"I'm not totally useless," he whispered back. "I've already told you that, silly girl."

"Thanks," she whispered again.

"Girl! You!" Madam Lewis turned round and pointed at Morag. "What did you say? Who are you talking to?"

"No one, Madam Lewis," said Morag.

"Good. If there's one thing I can't stand it is chatty girls. Now, follow me. After a small breakfast you can make a start on your chores."

15

The Lady Mephista was in her beautifully furnished bed-room, sitting at her dressing table gazing at her reflection in the huge mirror, when Madam Lewis brought in Morag and Chelsea. Morag gasped when she looked around her. She had never seen such a lavish room in her life.

Mephista's dressing table was gilded and ornately carved, and extremely old-looking—Morag guessed it was an antique. To the right stood the biggest four-poster bed she had ever seen. It was made of a dark wood—oak, Morag thought—and was furnished with gossamer drapes of the finest pink voile and covered in a beautiful pink silk quilt. On the pink silk pillows lay a battered moth-eaten teddy bear.

Over an intricately carved stone fireplace hung a pair of oil paintings of two of the saddest-looking people Morag had ever seen. One was of a woman who looked a bit like Mephista, except her hair was blond. The other was of a dark-haired man with a handsome face. Morag wondered briefly who they were.

The entire room smelled of an expensive but delicate perfume. If Morag had not been quite so intimidated by Mephista, she would have loved to spend all day there.

Lady Mephista did not seem to know they were there at first, and missed Madam Lewis's low bow and Chelsea's neat curtsy. She began to brush her long copper-colored hair while the three waited and Morag took the chance to study her.

She was a tall, thin young woman wearing a pale pink silk dressing gown and matching pale pink slippers. Gold earrings dangled from her ears and she wore a gleaming pearl and gold necklace around her graceful white throat. She was truly beautiful, Morag thought, but it was a kind of cold beauty that suggested Mephista was not always nice. A look of arrogance never left her dark, almost black eyes as she watched herself in the mirror. Morag sensed she was not a person to be trifled with.

Madam Lewis cleared her throat and bowed again. Mephista looked at her in the mirror. She had finally deigned to acknowledge their presence.

"Why have you disturbed me, Lewis?" asked Mephista in a soft, clear voice. "What do you want?"

"We're here to be at Your Ladyship's bidding," Madam

Lewis answered. "May we, with your permission, prepare your bath and help Your Ladyship dress for the day?"

In the mirror, Mephista smirked. "You may," she said, continuing to brush her hair. "But be sure you use the correct cleansing milk this time, Lewis. I won't be bathed in that muck again."

"Yes, Your Ladyship," replied Madam Lewis, bowing again. She backed off from Mephista, still bowing as she went and signaling to Morag and Chelsea to do the same.

"Wait!" cried Mephista.

Madam Lewis straightened and waited for her lady to speak. Mephista spun round on her chair. She looked straight at Morag, her emotionless dark eyes piercing the young girl's confidence. A feeling of vulnerability washed over Morag and she looked away, afraid the gaze would crush her.

"Who," asked Mephista starkly, "is that?" She pointed a perfectly manicured finger at Morag. The fingernail had been painted blood red.

"Your Ladyship, this is the new girl," replied Madam Lewis carefully. "She's here as a present from your father."

"My father?" queried Mephista in surprise. "But he's not here."

"No, Your Ladyship, but he left instructions before he went that you were to have another lady's maid," answered Madam Lewis. She bowed again.

"Oh, he did, did he? About time. I've been telling him for ages that I've been in need of another girl to help out. I mean, Arogona Bletchcock has three maids, so why shouldn't I? It wouldn't be fair if I were to be left with only

186

two—an old maid and a young idiot, like you two—now, would it?"

Madam Lewis visibly flinched at this—something that was lost on Mephista—but kept her cool. She merely replied: "No, ma'am."

"Is she strong? Is she trained? Does she have good manners and nice ways? I won't have another one like that awful girl we had before. What was her name again, Lewis?"

"Maclaine, ma'am."

"Yes, her. Stupid, freckly girl. Kept breaking things. You did get rid of her, didn't you, Lewis?"

"Yes, ma'am. She'll be no trouble now," replied Madam Lewis with an evil smirk. Morag saw the look and felt uneasy.

"Good. And this one? She's capable?"

"Yes, ma'am. She was a maid to royalty," lied Madam Lewis.

"Really?" Mephista seemed to like that. She was impressed. "Splendid." She turned to Morag. "What's your name?"

"Morag . . . er . . . ma'am," ventured Morag, her voice quavering slightly with nerves. Mephista was quite imposing.

"Come over here," demanded Mephista. Morag left Madame Lewis's side and walked over to stand directly in front of that thin, angular face. She felt too intimidated to look into the woman's eyes, so she focused on her tormentor's beautiful hair.

"Well, Morag," began Mephista. "You'd better live up

to Lewis's recommendation. Or else you'll go the way of that other girl. What was her name again, Lewis?"

"Maclaine, ma'am."

"Yes. You'll go the way of Maclaine before you, do you understand?" she said.

"What happened to Maclaine, ma'am?" asked Morag quietly.

"How dare you question Her Ladyship like that, girl!" scolded Madam Lewis. "Her Ladyship does not invite your questions."

"No, no." Mephista sneered. "I think it will do both these girls good to know what happens to wasteful people. Instead of reporting for duty one day, she went swimming. They found her body underneath the jetty several hours later." Her face registered regret, but Morag could tell Mephista didn't mean it.

"At least, they found parts of it," she added.

Mephista leaned forward and whispered in Morag's ear, "You don't want me to think you're a terrible waste as well, do you?"

"No, ma'am," mumbled Morag as she started to tremble with fear.

"I'm glad we understand each other," she said.

Then her mood changed as if someone had flicked a switch. "Lewis," she said, smiling. "Ready my bath. I have an important day ahead of me."

"Very good, ma'am."

At about the same time, out at sea, Kyle the Fisherman woke Bertie and Aldiss.

"Come and see this—it's unbelievable!" He pointed excitedly as the dodo and the rat rubbed the sleep out of their eyes.

Ahead, on the horizon, rose the dark towering cliff faces of an island that lay unseen by most mortals. It was that early part of the morning when there was light, but the sun had not yet risen. A white mist obscured the high hills of the island, but the storm had died and the wild seas around it were now relatively calm. The three stared at the island as it emerged through the low clouds and morning fog.

"Murst," Kyle whispered. "It's incredible. I mean, my father talked about it, but I wondered if such a place really existed. I never thought I'd ever see it for myself."

"Someone should wake Shona," suggested Aldiss.

"She wouldn't want to miss this," agreed Bertie. "This will be the first time she's seen her home in decades."

But they didn't have to wake her. Shona was already sitting up on the deck, gazing wistfully at the island where she was born. Tears stung her yellow eyes as she remembered how she had been tricked into leaving the island by Devlish, only to be trapped and turned to stone.

She had been the last pygmy dragon of Murst. The last one to have survived. And he had taken her life from her for thirty years. Anger burned in her heart as she remembered the sneer on Devlish's face as he cast the final spell that had kept her prisoner for so long. Shona closed her eyes and thought about all the nasty things she would like to do to Devlish when she caught up with him, and how she would punish him for what he had done. All sorts of horrible thoughts flew through her head, becoming more and more awful as they went on.

Then she realized that she was allowing her anger to overtake her and she made a conscious effort to relax. She breathed deeply, in and out, in and out, slowly calming the fire rising within. There was no point thinking about it just now, she thought, when there was a job to do. Her vengeance could wait.

She instructed Kyle to drop anchor for a while at the north side of the island, out of sight of the castle. They needed to go over their story again. They rehearsed what they were going to do and what they were going to say at least five times before everyone was happy.

"What are we going to do with that stinking Klapp demon while we're away?" Kyle, who didn't want the creature on board his boat, asked.

"He'll have to stay where he is, I'm afraid," replied Bertie. "We don't have any choice. He won't get out; he's shut in tight. But we'll have to make sure we've fastened the portholes tightly. It would be a disaster if he were to escape."

"Fine," said Kyle, a little grudgingly. He was not too happy about harboring the dirty creature any longer than he had to.

"Everyone ready?" Bertie asked nervously. Everyone nodded. "Okay, Kyle, take us round."

Kyle hoisted the anchor on board and started up the engine of the fishing boat. The engine sounded unnervingly loud as the boat chugged around the peninsula, past the imposing gray battlements of Murst Castle. It didn't take them long to arrive at the shoreline, and Kyle carefully docked the boat at the wooden pier.

There was a flurry of activity on the shore as the boat moored. The giant guards, who had been sleeping peacefully on the beach, all jumped to attention at the sound of the arrival of the fishing boat. They gathered up their pikes and swords and ran one after the other along the pier, their footsteps thundering along the planks. They lined up neatly in front of the boat.

One spoke: "Who goes there? What's your business on Murst?"

Kyle was busy bending over a wooden post as he tied up the boat.

"I am Kyle the Great," he said with a grin, straightening up. "And I have come here to buy supplies and to provide the most magical of entertainments to all within the great castle." He motioned toward the towers beyond with a theatrical sweep of his arm. It caused the already agitated guards to flinch.

"Entertainments? What *sort* of entertainments?" said the guard. He was a great ugly brute, with straggly hair and a wart on the end of his nose.

"Suspense is part of the fun, gentlemen," replied Kyle mysteriously. He leapt lightly from the boat onto the jetty. The guards all lowered their pikes in a threatening manner.

"And you wouldn't want me to ruin the fun for you, would you?" he went on. "I'm not here to do anything other than to amaze and entertain. Now, who's in charge of this great place? I need to speak to him."

"The Master's not here at present," said the guard. Bertie and Aldiss, who were hiding out in the bridge, sighed with relief. At least that was one evil person they didn't have to deal with.

"Well, who's in charge when he's not here?" Kyle asked.

"That'll be Her Ladyship you'll be wanting," replied the guard.

"Great, then I'll just gather up my creatures and you can take me to her."

"Creatures? What *kind* of creatures?" The guard looked uneasy. "Think you'd better leave your creatures on board your boat, sir. For health and safety reasons."

"And disappoint the Lady?" replied Kyle the Fisherman coolly. "I don't think so. Give me a minute. It won't take me long to unload them. Why don't you tell this lot to go on up to the castle and we'll be along presently?"

The guard, taken aback by Kyle's confidence, did so and followed his fellow troops up the hill toward the castle gates, where they waited impatiently at the great doorway for this stranger and his mysterious creatures.

Kyle jumped back onto his boat and pulled the tarpaulin off Shona, then called Bertie and Aldiss to come out from their hiding places.

"Let's go, we're on!"

Bertie, Aldiss and Shona scrambled off the boat and followed the fisherman up to the castle. Kyle did his best to be confident, and strutted up to the gates like he owned the place, but inside he was feeling tense and a little worried. If this plan was to go wrong, they would be in grave danger. He wasn't the only one to be concerned. The others were equally nervous, so much so that the little rat couldn't even speak. Presently, the four met the guards at the great gates of Murst Castle. Kyle looked at the first one expectantly.

"Well, aren't you going to let us in?" he demanded in a loud voice.

The first guard looked at his fellow guards and there was a bit of whispering between them.

"I'm *waiting*," said Kyle with mock impatience.

There was some more whispering and then the first guard spoke again.

"Very well, follow me," he said. "I'll take you to the main hall. But I'm warning you, if there's any trouble, you'll never see daylight again."

He eyed Shona suspiciously. "Shouldn't that thing be tied up or muzzled or something?"

Shona glowered at the guard and opened her mouth to reply, but was stopped by Kyle, who held up a hand and patted her lightly on the snout.

"No, not necessary," he said warmly. "She's very well trained. It's the bird you've got to watch."

On cue, Bertie crowed and snapped his beak at the guard. The guard blinked in surprise, looked at Bertie closely and then shrugged.

"I'm sure I can handle a budgie," he said with a snort of laughter. Bertie frowned. "Especially one as stupid-looking as that one." He chuckled, and his fellow guards erupted into laughter. Kyle glowered at them all.

"I'll have you know that that bird is the extremely rare and ferocious Wooka Wooka bird of Papua New Guinea," he lied. "It'll have your head off as soon as look at you," he continued. Bertie tried his best to look fierce and obviously succeeded because all the guards were eyeing him with a new wariness.

"Oh!" said the first guard, knocking loudly on the door of the castle. He looked at Bertie again, this time with a little trepidation in his eyes. "Well, shouldn't he be tied or caged or something?"

"No need," replied Kyle. "I have him well trained also."

The great wooden door of the castle swung slowly open and the guards ushered them inside. They led them into the outer cobbled courtyard, where there was another grand wooden doorway that led to the hallway decorated with weapons and tapestries, where Morag herself had been the night before. They were taken through the door at the end of the corridor and into the largest room any of them had ever seen.

Fires raged in the grates of three immense stone fireplaces. In front of them a vast oak table laden with breads and fruit spanned the length of the Great Hall of Murst Castle. Low oak benches lined the table and at the far end, on one of two golden thrones, sat the Lady of the Castle, Mephista.

Although they were some distance from her, the friends could see she was something to behold. Dressed in a tight-fitting blue velvet gown, and wearing an impressive gold and pearl necklace, her long red hair hanging in ringlets around her face, Mephista was magnificent to look at. Kyle's jaw wasn't the only one to drop. Bertie and Aldiss, who peered out from behind him, looked like they were catching flies too. Shona, who was never impressed by other females, rolled her eyes in disgust at the way her friends were acting. It was as if they had never seen a woman before.

"Who comes to my castle at this early hour?" Mephista called. Her voice was musical and light. "Come closer so that I might see you better."

Led by the first guard, they walked the length of the table and were halted about ten paces from where Mephista sat. On the table before her, on large golden platters, lay the remnants of her breakfast of bread and honey. A golden chalice was held in her right hand. She sipped from it as she surveyed the man, the dragon, the dodo and the rat. Her face said "impress me," so Kyle did his best. He bowed deeply.

"My Lady," he began. "My name is Kyle the Great, and we come to your island seeking hospitality and to provide entertainment that will amaze and amuse."

Mephista, who had been lounging back on her throne, sat forward.

"Amaze and amuse, eh?" she said. "And how will you do that, minstrel?"

"Not me, ma'am, but my creatures. If you would be so

generous and kind as to provide us with some food and water, we will put on a show tonight for all the people in this castle, a show that you will never forget."

"And why should I do that?" she replied. "None of you look like anything special. What can you do that's so different?"

Kyle smiled. "Ma'am, we have played for kings and queens across Earth. We have performed for prime ministers and presidents across the globe. We are famous from Peru to Paisley. Surely a sophisticated lady like yourself must have heard of us?"

Now Mephista, who considered herself the epitome of fashion in the magical world, did not want to admit that she had never heard of Kyle the Great and his animals. She prided herself on being up-to-date on what was currently in fashion, and wondered how she could have missed this one.

"How do I know you are telling the truth?" she asked, watching Kyle's face very closely for any signs of evasion.

"Your Ladyship, let us perform tonight and you will see why we are so in demand in every country. All we ask is that you provide a little hospitality."

She thought for a moment. Her father wasn't due home for another day and she had become very bored with castle life. They seemed harmless enough, and if they stepped out of line there were plenty of ways to torture them. Even if they didn't step out of line, she might torture them anyway. She smiled.

"All right," she said. "You can stay. Guard, take them

down to the kitchen and instruct Cook to feed them," she commanded before she turned her attention back to Kyle. "Well, Kyle the Great," she said. "I hope your show is as good as you've promised. Otherwise I will not be happy." She leaned a little closer to the fisherman. "And you would not want to make me unhappy!"

Kyle returned her gaze confidently. "Trust me, Your Ladyship, you'll not regret your decision."

Mephista did not reply to this, merely waved her hand, indicating that their conversation was over and the guard was to take them away.

The four were led downstairs into a large kitchen, where Kyle was offered a seat at a small table, and the three animals (much to Shona's disgust, because she snorted at the suggestion of it) were told to lie on the floor. Bertie thumped Shona on the hide as a warning for her not to say anything and she stayed quiet and lay down. The guard, who had other duties to perform in the castle that morning, warned Kyle that he and his animals had to behave and told him that he'd be back later. With barely a nod, the guard left them in the care of the cook and her four kitchen staff, three girls and a sullen boy.

The cook was an ordinary-looking human woman with ruddy cheeks and a sad expression. She silently placed a bowl of thick porridge down in front of Kyle and he thanked her. From their place on the floor, Bertie, Aldiss and Shona licked their lips greedily. They hadn't eaten since the night before and they were all feeling attacks of sharp hunger pangs. Bertie, who still had his satchel, dared

197

not use it in case anyone saw. Thankfully, Kyle was very aware of their needs and turned to Cook, who was back at the great porridge pot that bubbled merrily on the old iron stove.

"What about my animals?" he asked her as she stirred the giant pot with a great big wooden spurtle (which is a kind of stick you stir porridge with).

"What about them?" she asked quietly. "I only feed men and giants," she said. "Not animals."

"They would eat some porridge too," he said.

"Not in my kitchen," said Cook. "I don't like creatures in my kitchen. Not unless they are already dead and ready for cooking."

The kitchen boy sniggered. Kyle threw him a dirty look.

"My animals need feeding," he said firmly. "Please furnish them with some porridge and some milk. We are here to entertain Her Ladyship tonight and I don't want to have to tell her we did not receive the proper welcome she had promised."

Cook pursed her lips, looked at Kyle, then the animals, and back at Kyle again.

"I suppose," she said slowly, "I could spare them some porridge and milk."

Kyle flashed her a smile.

"Thank you."

"Grain," she said to the boy. "Wipe that stupid smile off your face, boy, and go and feed the animals some porridge, will you?"

"Aw, Mum, why me? Why not the girls? It's always me that's got to do the nasty work." Grain whined. " 'S'not fair." He eyed the dragon warily. Shona glowered back at him. She loved intimidating nasty boys.

"Grain, just do as you're told and give me peace. I've got work to do. The Master's coming back soon and I need to prepare." His mother sighed.

At this, Bertie started. Devlish was returning here? Soon? How soon? He hoped Kyle had the audacity to ask and he wasn't disappointed.

"Your Master's coming home?" said Kyle innocently. "Will he be here tonight to see our show? How wonderful!" He feigned excitement. "We've always wanted to play before the Great Devlish. I was disappointed to learn he wasn't here, but now I know he's returning, that's really good news."

The cook snorted.

"He'll not be back tonight," she said. "At least, not this evening. So you won't get to perform for him. Disappointed you again, have I?"

"Oh!" Kyle sighed, trying to act disappointed, even though he was secretly relieved. "So, when's he back?"

"I don't know. The Master never tells us exactly when. All I know is that he'll be back by lunchtime tomorrow, maybe before then. I've to have food prepared for him anyway." She turned to her son. "Grain, come and feed those animals now, boy. I won't be telling you again!"

Reluctantly, the boy shuffled over to his mother. He picked up three large bowls from a pile that had been drying next to the sink and handed them to his mother one after the other. She filled each with porridge and handed them back. Carefully, carrying one at a time, the boy took the bowls of porridge over to where Shona, Bertie and Aldiss were sitting on the cold stone floor and placed them in front of them, then scarpered back to the safety of his mother.

As Grain had not given them spoons, the three animals ate directly from the bowls. They tucked into the food eagerly. Going without cutlery went against Bertie's sensibilities, for he was a cultured bird, but he shrugged off his discomfort and buried his beak in the bowl.

"I ask you," continued Cook. "Is it fair to ask someone as skilled as me in the kitchen to prepare something for when the Master returns and not tell me when to expect him? How can I have something hot ready for him when I don't know when he'll be here? It's ridiculous," she said, throwing down the spurtle. She took up an oven glove and opened the oven door to check on whatever was cooking inside. A blast of heat filled the kitchen.

"So true, so true," agreed Kyle as he finished his porridge. "Madam, that was a fine bowl of porridge. I'm sure anything you prepare for the Master will be welcomed, hot or cold."

Cook closed the oven door and looked at him suspiciously, as if she were trying to work out what he was playing at. Kyle gave her his best grin and patted his stomach.

"Delicious," he said, smiling.

She returned the smile. "Would you like some more?" she asked.

"I couldn't possibly," replied Kyle, holding his hands up. "I'm stuffed full to the gills." He pushed his chair back and stood up. "And will you be cooking dinner for to-night?" he asked, scooping his plate up and taking it over to the sink, where one of the girls was up to her elbows in foamy water doing the dishes. He deposited the plate in the sink and gave the girl a cheeky wink. She giggled nervously.

Cook nodded. "Me and some others," she said. "But I'm in charge down here. It's my kitchen."

"Of course," said Kyle. "So what will you be making? If it's anything near as delicious as your porridge, dinner will be a big success."

"As it always is," said Cook, pleased with Kyle's flattering words. "I'll be cooking up some broth, roast pig and apple pie and custard for afters."

"Sounds delicious, I can't wait to try it," he said. He looked round at the others and saw that they too had finished. "Well," he said. "I'd best be off. Got to rest my animals before the big show tonight. Thank you for the lovely breakfast." He gave her another smile, took her right hand and kissed it.

"Until tonight," he said. "After dinner . . . you will be coming to our show, won't you?"

Cook giggled nervously and smiled. "Of course," she said. "I wouldn't miss it."

16

"What was all *that* about?" Bertie demanded when they were alone in a room somewhere at the back of the castle. It was sparsely furnished, with white walls, a single bed and a rickety wicker chair. It smelled dusty, as though no one had stayed in it for a very long time. The guard had deposited them there only a couple of minutes earlier, instructing Kyle that he and his animals could "room in there for the night." Bertie climbed up on to the bed and made himself as comfortable as he could against two very flat pillows.

"What was *what* about?" asked Kyle, looking at the bird with a puzzled expression on his face.

"The stuff about the food and how good it was?" Bertie said. "Personally, I thought the porridge tasted burnt."

"Me too!" piped up Aldiss from the corner. He had scampered up one of the legs of the wicker chair and was perched quite comfortably on the arm.

"Yes," said Shona, lying on the floor, her back legs and tail hanging out of the door and into the corridor. The room wasn't quite big enough to accommodate the dragon and all the furniture. "Why the compliments?"

Kyle smiled. "To get information," he said. "I thought a bit of sweet-talking might encourage the cook to let slip some things and she did."

"Like what?" asked Aldiss, his tiny face contorted into a frown. "All I heard was stuff about food and how great you thought it would taste."

"Ah, yes, but what we were told was that Devlish was not coming back until tomorrow, which gives us enough time tonight to look for Morag and steal the Eye."

"Yes, but how are we going to do that now?" asked Bertie. "There are hundreds of guards in the castle."

"Well, that's where the food comes in. Tonight, before the meal is served, we're going to slip some sleeping potion into the soup and, once everyone is fast asleep, then we'll strike!" Kyle said triumphantly.

"Sounds like a good plan," said Shona, shifting into a sitting position. "But there's one fatal flaw."

"And what's that?" demanded Kyle.

Shona sighed and rolled her great yellow eyes. "Where on earth are you going to find a sleeping potion?"

"Ah . . . well, I was hoping Bertie might come up with some of that from his magic satchel," he replied, looking hopefully at the dodo. Bertie held his satchel protectively in his wings and shook his head.

"I don't think I can," he said. "It's a magic satchel, true enough, but I've never asked it for something like that. I don't think it's capable of producing ready-made magic potions. In fact, I'm sure of it."

Kyle scratched his chin thoughtfully.

"If it can't come up with the actual potion, can it magic up the ingredients?" he asked.

"I'm not sure. I suppose I could try." The dodo took the satchel from his shoulder and opened it. He paused. "What are the ingredients I need?" he asked quietly.

"Don't you know?" asked Shona in surprise.

"But you're top of the class for magic!" squeaked Aldiss.

"I . . . well, I'm not *quite* top of the class," Bertie admitted. "I sort of embellished that one," he said. "I'm more . . . well, I'm more toward the middle."

Shona's eyes closed into slits, making her look all the more menacing.

"What do you mean 'toward the middle'?" she asked.

Bertie looked a little embarrassed.

"I'm not at the *bottom* of the class," he assured them. "But I'm not at the top either. I'm sort of middling in all my magical subjects . . . except, that is, well . . ."

"Except for potions?" Shona asked. The dodo nodded.

"I'm not terribly good at potions," the bird admitted, blushing under his feathers.

"Well, why did Montgomery ask you to free me?" she

demanded. She looked a little upset. "Why did he choose *you* if you are as average as you say you are?"

"He didn't actually ask me to do anything," Bertie admitted and Aldiss squeaked in shock. The dodo went on, "I overheard him speaking to Madam Guthrie, the Enchantments Mistress at Marnoch Mor College, about the Eye of Lornish and Shona, and I sort of took it upon myself . . . to . . . well . . . I thought that if I could get the Eye back and free Shona, then Montgomery might think me a good wizard and . . . and that's about it. . . ." His voice trailed off. He sighed. "I stole the runes and the enchantment and I talked Aldiss into coming with me and I'm sorry, but . . . Oh! Oh!"

Great tears rolled down his feathery cheeks. "I just wanted to do something well for a change," he confessed. "Something that would make me stand out. I'm so sorry I lied to you all."

They all sat in an uncomfortable silence. No one could look at the dodo, although Kyle did offer him a handkerchief.

"Look," said Kyle kindly. "No harm done, eh?"

"No harm done? No HARM?" spluttered Shona indignantly. "He's brought us on a false mission and put us in harm's way!"

"He freed you from that hilltop," Kyle reminded her. Shona was silent. "And now we're here to find Morag and Henry, and we still have to get the Eye back anyway. So let's forget about what Bertie has done and think about how we can make this sleeping potion, because I can't think of any other way to do this."

They all fell silent for a while, each lost in their own thoughts, brows furrowed into frowns as they tried to come up with a plan. Then, after what seemed like an age, Aldiss let out a little squeak of excitement.

"Bertie?" he asked. "Can that bag conjure up *anything*?"

"Well, I've only really asked it for food so far," began the dodo.

"Why don't you ask it for a sleeping potion spell?"

"Now why didn't I think of that?" said Shona dryly.

"I don't think so," said the bird, still unsure.

"Just ask!" Shona, Kyle and Aldiss exclaimed together. The dodo shrugged and muttered something about there being "nothing to lose." He closed his eyes, whispered gently to the bag, put his wing inside, and to his surprise pulled out a piece of parchment. Excitedly, he unrolled it and began to read.

"Well?" asked Kyle.

The dodo shook his head. "I can't look," he said.

Aldiss took it from him. "It looks like some kind of recipe," he said. "It's no use, Bertie!"

"Give me that!" said Shona, and she snatched the paper and began to read. As she read, a big smile began to play on her lips, making her look—to anyone who might have been outside looking in—truly sinister and ferocious. Her sharp, flesh-tearing teeth glittered nastily.

"This, you dope, is the recipe for a sleeping potion. We need a couple of bits and pieces, but I think we can make it." She looked around the room. "We need a fire, though."

There was a small, unlit grate in the corner and a pile of logs in a basket off to the side.

"Perfect." Shona smiled. She inhaled, then remembered she hadn't quite told the truth the day before. She turned to Kyle.

"While we're at it, I also have a confession, Kyle," she began. "I wasn't totally honest with you the other day. I *can* breathe fire. I'm also sorry I lied."

The fisherman shrugged and then looked at Aldiss.

"Any important secrets you've got to share with us?" he asked.

The rat thought for a moment. "The smell on the boat wasn't just the Klapp demon," he said in a little voice.

"Good grief," muttered Bertie, ruffling his feathers.

"Well, unless there's anything else?" said Kyle, nodding to Shona. "I suppose we'd better put all this behind us and get started on that potion. We've got a girl and a stone to rescue."

Elsewhere in the castle, Morag was finding being a maid for Mephista to be heavy work. If it hadn't been for the fact that she had her medallion for company, she would have found the experience extremely depressing. Henry kept her spirits up by making silly comments about the other servants and about Mephista herself.

"What are you sniggering at?" demanded Chelsea as the two girls helped Madam Lewis prepare Mephista's gown for that evening's dinner. The dress was made of a deep plum-colored silk. Morag loved the feel of the soft fabric passing through her hands.

"Nothing," she said, stifling a giggle. She was laughing at Henry's calling Madam Lewis "a scratchy twig."

"Hmm," replied Chelsea, not convinced. A conspiratorial look appeared on her face. "Have you heard?" she whispered loudly enough for everyone else to hear. "We're in for a treat tonight."

"What do you mean?" asked Morag, whose only idea of a treat was to escape from the castle.

"Apparently, there's some animal trainer in the castle. And you'll never guess what he's brought with him."

Morag smoothed the folds of Mephista's dress down and helped Madam Lewis lay it on Her Ladyship's great four-poster bed.

"What?" asked Morag, not really that interested.

"Only a dragon and a dodo!" cried Chelsea triumphantly. "Oh, and a rat, too, but I hate rats, so I won't be looking at him."

"A dragon?" asked Morag, suddenly animated. "And a dodo and rat?" Morag's heart leapt into her mouth and she was temporarily struck dumb with excitement. They had come to rescue her!

"Yeah, they're going to do some sort of performance after dinner, the castle's buzzing with it. S'not often we get entertainers here on account of the fact no one from the mainland can find the place. It'll be brilliant. It's dead boring round here normally," Chelsea prattled on. But Morag didn't hear. All she could think about was finding her friends and getting out of this place and back to . . . but where would she go back to? She didn't want to live with Jermy and Moira again. She didn't really have anywhere *to* go. She decided to worry about *that* after she was rescued.

". . . and it's quite fierce, although the man's not bad-looking, according to Sadie down in the kitchens," Chelsea continued. "Are you listening to me, Morag?"

"Morag couldn't help but listen," snapped Madam Lewis. "In fact, I'm sure the whole castle heard you going on and on about these entertainers. Just be quiet and get on with your work. Fetch me Her Ladyship's shoes."

Chelsea didn't speak again and did as she was told. She went to a large chest and heaved the lid open. As she rummaged through the assorted pairs of shoes inside, Morag was still rooted to the spot by the bed, absentmindedly stroking the dress, her thoughts lost in her dream of being rescued.

"You, girl!" growled Madam Lewis, snapping Morag back out of her musings. "Stop daydreaming and go and tidy Her Ladyship's dressing table."

"Yes, Madam Lewis," said Morag automatically. She hurried over to the large ornate dressing table with its large mirror and began to work. As she tidied and polished, Morag wondered where her friends were in the castle and who this mysterious man was who was with them. Perhaps, she thought, some evil man had kidnapped them like her and was making them perform for money. The idea suddenly terrified her. If that was the case, they were all prisoners now on this bleak secret island.

Around an hour later, Madam Lewis, in a fit of unchar-acteristic generosity, allowed the girls to have some time to themselves before dinner. She told them she expected them to return to the bedroom in exactly one hour to help Her Ladyship dress for the evening.

"Do not be late, Her Ladyship hates anyone being late," she warned.

"Yes, Madam Lewis," chorused the girls, each bobbing into a curtsy.

"So," said Morag as the girls made their way to their tower bedroom. "Where in the castle are these performers staying?" She tried to keep her voice light so as not to arouse Chelsea's suspicions, but Chelsea by her very nature was a suspicious girl.

"Why?" she demanded.

The girls traipsed along a corridor from the bedcham-bers and down a winding staircase to the back of the castle.

"Just wondered where they would keep a dragon safely in the castle, that was all," said Morag airily.

"You're a terrible liar," said Chelsea. "I know exactly the reason why you want to know."

Fear gripped Morag's throat tightly.

"You do?" she asked hesitantly. "And what's that?"

"You're wanting to see what a real live dragon looks like. I bet you've never seen one," taunted Chelsea.

"Bet *you* haven't," retorted Morag.

"Bet I have!"

"Where?"

"Well, I can't quite remember where cos it was a long time ago and I was only wee, but I definitely saw one."

"You are such a fibber, Chelsea," said Morag, opening a small door out into the courtyard. It had been raining steadily all afternoon and their feet slipped and slid over the wet cobbles.

"Don't call me that, you stupid girl," snarled Chelsea. "I *have* seen one, I tell you."

"Yeah, right!" Morag opened another door that led into the servants' tower, at the top of which was their room. She followed Chelsea down the stairs into the large kitchen.

"I *have* seen a dragon, and it looked," Chelsea went on, ". . . exactly like that!" Stumbling through the door into the kitchen, Morag immediately recognized Shona lying peacefully in the corner. Her heart leapt with joy.

Shona raised her head and looked at the two girls. She did not seem to know Morag and the girl was temporarily crushed, but said nothing. Maybe, it occurred to her, Shona *had* recognized her but was not letting on; perhaps it was part of a plan. She followed Chelsea into the kitchen and saw a man sitting at the table, eating bread and cheese. He looked very happy with himself.

"That your dragon, mister?" asked Chelsea cheekily.

"Yes, what of it?" he answered lazily.

"Can I stroke it?"

"I don't think she'd like strangers touching her," said Kyle. "She's ferocious when she gets going."

Chelsea looked both impressed and a little fearful, but her bold nature pushed her on. She took a chair next to Kyle and sat down, striking up a conversation with the fisherman about where he was from and what he was doing on Murst.

Kyle, who was conscious of not letting his guard down, lied to the young girl, telling her made-up tales of his life as a traveling minstrel. While they talked, Morag crept up to Shona. Behind the dragon, she could see the slumbering bodies of Bertie and Aldiss, sitting upright, heads resting on Shona's flank, fast asleep. The dragon's great yellow eyes bored through Morag.

"Shona, it's me!" whispered Morag. She looked over anxiously to where Kyle and Chelsea were still deep in conversation. At the stove, the cook was preparing that night's dinner, the kitchen maids were gossiping at the sink and a lanky boy was peeling spuds at another table. None of them were watching her.

"I know," the dragon whispered back, grinning. "We've come to get you."

It was the news Morag had longed for, but she covered up her smile.

"Can't talk," continued the dragon in a whisper. "Just don't eat the soup!"

"What?"

"Don't eat the soup!" With a flick of her head, Shona motioned to Morag that danger was around. She said nothing more, merely rested her head on her front claws and closed her eyes. Morag looked at her, stunned.

"Did she just say what I thought she said?" she whispered to Henry.

"She said not to eat the soup," answered the magical medallion from under her uniform.

"What do you think that means?" asked Morag, who couldn't see what the soup had to do with her rescue.

"That you shouldn't eat the soup," replied the medallion.

"Hoi, you two! Out!" shouted the cook from the stove. She had had enough of kids coming through her kitchen to see the dragon, and besides, as she was quite taken with the charming dragon tamer, she wanted him to herself.

Chelsea scrambled to her feet, said a curt "bye" to Kyle and motioned for Morag to follow her out. The pair ran across the kitchen floor, their shoes making clumping noises as they went. Chelsea yanked open the door to the tower and disappeared inside the stairwell. With the quickest of grateful glances back to her friends, Morag followed. Breathlessly, they ran upstairs to their room, with Chelsea full of new information to share about her discussions with Kyle.

As she sat on her bed, Morag listened to the girl's excited prattle and smiled. They were coming to get her, she thought. She was going to be rescued after all.

17

When dinner was announced, it seemed like the entire population of the castle made its way to the Great Hall. It was only early evening, but it was already dark outside, and the huge hall was lit by large flaming torches placed at regular intervals around the walls and from the glow of hundreds of white candles wavering on the many heavy silver candelabras on the tables. The tables were laid out in an H shape, and were covered by pristine white tablecloths, silver cutlery and delicate china.

Kyle, Shona, Bertie and Aldiss watched from the shadows by the door as twenty or so ermine-clad ladies of the castle and their partners took the more comfortable dining chairs at the long table that made the crossbar of the H. The rest of the diners—guards, the more senior servants and some others—sat on benches at the tables placed either side.

Mephista and the most senior of her courtiers took their places at the top table, which sat on a separate platform overlooking the other tables. There were about six seats at the top table, and in the center were two golden thrones, on one of which Mephista gracefully sat down.

The noise in the Great Hall was deafening. The high ceilings and ancient stones created incredible echoes, which were bad enough when there were a handful of people in the room but truly dreadful when, as there was that night, there were at least two hundred there. As the diners took their seats, their shoes slapped hard on the gray flagstone floor and the wood screeched across the stone as they pulled the benches and chairs out to sit down. Eventually, the chatter of the diners quieted down and servants appeared to serve the first glasses of wine of the evening.

Mephista, looking grand in her deep plum silk gown, smiled majestically at her assorted courtiers from her seat at the top table and chatted amiably to her advisers on either side. A servant nervously approached the great lady and said something to her before bowing very low. Mephista nodded and then motioned for the servant to go away, which he did as quickly as his legs could carry him.

Mephista apparently had instructed him to begin serving the first course, for a stream of servants reappeared carrying steaming bowls of soup. A female servant, carrying five bowls of soup on a large wooden tray, passed very

215

close to where Kyle and the others stood watching. She served her soup to the guards sitting nearby, before turning about and walking straight past the waiting friends. But then she stopped dead in her tracks. She looked at them, wondering why they weren't seated or eating.

"Aren't you sitting down for some dinner?" she asked Kyle. He recognized her as one of the cook's daughters.

"No, we'll get some later. Can you ask your mother to save us some?" he asked. "We can get it after the show."

The girl smiled and nodded. She disappeared through a side door, which led straight down to the kitchen.

"Can any of you see Morag yet?" whispered Aldiss, straining to see the young girl.

"No, she's not here," said Shona.

"But she knows about the soup?" asked Bertie.

"Yes—shh, someone will hear," replied Shona in a whisper. She looked fearfully over to where two guards were staring at them. She gave them the briefest of fake snorts before looking away and pretending to sniff Aldiss. The rat, who hated being sniffed, gave her a stinker of a look and moved away.

They watched as the diners greedily ate their soup. Then, as the plates were cleared by the servants, one by one the diners started to yawn, stretch and eventually doze off, a few sitting bolt upright on their benches, swaying gently from side to side, others putting their heads in their hands and lying down on the table. Some slumped quietly in their chairs, and many snored loudly.

The people sitting at the top table were the last to pass

out. The friends were pleased to see that everyone had become affected by the sleeping potion, but they didn't wait to see them all drop off—they didn't have time. Instead, they began the next stage of the plan: to find Morag.

They didn't have to look very far.

"So that's why you said not to touch the soup," said a voice on the other side of Shona. The friends all jumped in fright. Shona growled and turned to look at who it was and came face to face with a relieved Morag.

"Morag!" cried Bertie joyfully. He bounced over the dragon and landed at Morag's feet. He hugged her legs. "We're so pleased to see you!"

"Not as pleased as I am to see you. I didn't fancy being a slave here forever. It was almost as bad as living with Jermy and Moira."

"What exactly happened to you?" Aldiss asked, his little whiskers quivering with excitement.

"Well . . . ," she started.

"We'll have enough time to swap stories later," said Shona curtly. "We need to get going. We have to find the Eye."

"Who's this?" Morag asked, pointing to Kyle.

"I'm Kyle," replied the fisherman. "I was only supposed to get them here, but for some reason I'm in on the rescue mission now."

"Ahem," said the dragon meaningfully. She was anxious to get going.

"Okay, we'll talk later," said Kyle. "For now, we must find the Eye and get out of here. Morag? Any ideas?"

Morag thought for a moment. She hadn't seen much of the castle in the short time she had been there, but there was one place that Chelsea had mentioned earlier that might just be where the Eye was being kept.

"On the other side of the courtyard is the entrance to the tallest tower in the castle," she said. "There are a lot of guards, so Chelsea said. She said she didn't know what was in there, but it must be precious for Devlish to have so many people guarding it. She's been here nearly her whole life, so she would know. She said she once got into the tower, but was stopped by the Captain, who chased her out. Do you think the Eye might be in there?"

"Sounds like it," Bertie said, his feathery face pulled into a frown as he thought about it. "It's as good a place as any to start looking."

"But how will we get past the guards?" Morag wanted to know.

"You'll take them some soup with the compliments of the cook," said Kyle with a grin.

"Me? But I can't do that!" she protested. "I don't want to do it. What if they find out? What if they know?"

"You'll be fine," Kyle assured her. He patted her on the arm. "There's no way they'll suspect you, that's why I suggested you do it. Who would think a young girl like you would harm anyone?"

"Harm? What's in that soup? I thought it was sleeping potion!" squeaked Morag.

"It is," replied Kyle. "Morag, we really need you to do this. It's the only way."

Morag looked from Kyle to Bertie to Aldiss to Shona. They were all looking at her expectantly. Their four pairs of eyes pleaded with her to say yes. Despite her fears and the uncomfortable racing of her heart, Morag agreed to do it. Kyle was right, she realized; there was no other way.

Getting it from the kitchen was easy. The servants and cooking staff had also eaten the affected soup and were all snoozing quietly downstairs. The big pot was still bubbling on the stove, and Shona helped Morag ladle it into half a dozen wooden bowls. They stacked them on two trays and Morag and Kyle carefully carried them upstairs.

Anyone watching the proceedings at this moment would have seen a very peculiar sight—a young girl struggling with a tray full of steaming soup, followed by a tall dark man. He, in turn, was followed by a large green dragon, a gray dodo and, at the back, its whiskers twitching with excitement and fear, a little brown rat with extremely bright black eyes. One after the other they walked up the stairs, across the Great Hall and out through the wooden doors into the courtyard.

Treading carefully, so as not to slip on the cobbles, Morag and the others walked toward the largest tower at the other side. It was dark by now and very cold, and Morag was regretting that she had not thought to put on a coat. The night air was fresh with the smell of the sea, and Morag could just about see the faint outline of the moon as it hid behind a small cloud. As they approached the tower, the animals left the line and hid in the shadows of the castle walls, leaving Morag and Kyle to continue onward.

The tower was indeed as imposing as Morag had suggested and had only one entrance—a large steel door guarded by two sinister and heavily armored giants. They eyed her suspiciously as she approached them. Morag, who had been coached by Kyle on what to say, gave them a nervous smile.

"Good evening," she said. "Cook sent over some soup to warm you up. She said it was a right cold night and she was feeling sorry for you."

"Cook said that?" asked one of the guards incredulously. "That doesn't sound much like her. What's happened to her? Did she take a bump to the head?"

"I'd like to be the one that done that," said the other guard with a snigger. "Can't stand Cook, and she don't like me."

"Me neither," said the first guard. "She called me an outsized idiot the other day just cos I asked for a drink of lemonade." He turned to Morag and Kyle again, a great big frown on his face. "You sure she sent it?"

Morag nodded. "Yes, sir. She said she wanted to be nicer to everyone."

"She did?" asked the first guard, rubbing his stubbly chin with a giant hand. He bent over and looked more closely at the soup. It looked delicious. He sniffed. It smelled delicious. It was ages until they would get something to eat, and it was getting colder. He could do with something to warm him up. He picked up a bowl and a spoon and began to eat.

"What's it taste like, Sid?" the second guard asked, licking his lips.

"Delicious, Ken," replied the first.

"Dig in, before it gets cold," said Kyle. The second guard did as he was told and soon was shoveling soup into his large, tooth-filled mouth.

"May we pass soup on to your colleagues?" Kyle asked. The first guard yawned and rubbed his eyes.

"We're not supposed to let anyone in," he said. He had a good look at them. "But since you're being so generous, on you go." He turned to the other guard. "Do you know, I always feel the need of a nap after some good food."

"Me too, Sid," said Ken, and to back his statement up, yawned loudly.

"I think I'll just have a wee sit-down here," said Sid, sitting down in the doorway. "And rest my legs for five minutes."

"Me too," said Ken, sitting down beside him. They both rested their backs on the doorframe and were soon fast asleep. Morag looked at Kyle in astonishment. Kyle's plan was working.

"Let's get moving," said Kyle. "There's no time to lose."

He whistled to Bertie, Aldiss and Shona and they jumped from the shadows. Shona pushed open the heavy metal door for Morag and Kyle to enter. As the animals waited in the doorway, Morag and Kyle dispensed the rest of the soup to the four guards inside, and before long Morag appeared back at the door.

"Let's go," she said.

Inside, the tower was dimly lit by evenly spaced torches. The first room was circular and housed two large desks at which sat two slumbering guards. They snored loudly as the friends tiptoed past to a stairwell at the back. Carefully, they climbed the narrow spiral staircase, going round and round and round until they all felt quite dizzy. At last they came to a landing where there lay two more guards, empty soup plates discarded at their feet and their snores echoing thunderously down the passageway.

"Where to now?" asked Shona.

"We keep going up," said Kyle, pointing to another flight of stairs behind the guards.

And so they continued to climb, and Morag's legs ached as she went up another step and another and another. She was exhausted by the time they finally reached the landing at the top. Her legs were achy and wobbly and she had to sit down on a step for a short time to get her breath back. Her friends were all in a similar state.

Ahead of them stretched a small dingy hallway in which were two identical doors leading who-knew-where.

Morag looked at her friends nervously.

Now what? their faces said.

18

"Which one?" Bertie asked Morag as the five friends looked at the two doors. "Did Chelsea say?"

"No." She shrugged. "I don't know which one."

They stood in the little hallway and stared at the doors as if that alone would give them a clue as to what was behind them. The brass-handled doors were identical. They were arched and made from dark polished wood and embellished with swirling brass inlay. But which one to open? What if they opened one and unleashed whatever was concealed within?

At last, Kyle made a decision. He strode up to the door closer to them and gave it a yank. It swung open with a groan and Kyle gave a yelp of surprise and jumped back.

Two mops and a brush fell out and clattered on the wooden floor.

"It's not that door, then," Shona said with a laugh. Morag helped Kyle pick up the mops and brush and put them back in.

All attention turned to the other door. For a few moments, nobody moved.

Morag stepped forward and pulled the door open. Light flooded down into the dingy hallway, silhouetting her in the doorway. Everyone drew back, arms shielding their eyes, momentarily blinded by the strength of the dazzling light. As their eyes grew accustomed to the glare, they noticed a step leading to another flight of stairs.

"Come on," said Bertie, taking charge. "This must be the way." He hopped inside and disappeared into the brilliance of the light. They heard him clatter up the second stairwell, which, they soon found out, led to the highest part of the tower. Without hesitation, they followed him upward and began the final ascent.

Forty-one, forty-two, forty-three stairs, counted Morag. Forty-four and they were at the top and standing in a round room with no windows. The light came from a large white stone set on top of a wooden staff that floated in the middle of the room. There was a faint pulsing sound that seemed to be coming from the stone.

"The Eye of Lornish!" Bertie gasped. "It's so beautiful." He stared at it, mesmerized. "It's so much more beautiful than I thought it would be."

Aldiss, who was equally entranced by it, said nothing,

but stood whimpering quietly to himself. Morag had never seen anything like it before, had never dreamed that anything so exquisite could exist in this world. She felt herself being drawn toward the stone, desperate to touch it, to feel it in her hand and, as though in a trance, she felt herself move quietly forward, hand outstretched. If she could just touch it for a second . . .

"Stop!" Shona grabbed hold of her and pulled her back. "That stone is dangerous. We don't know what it could do to us."

"And if I know Devlish," said Bertie, "he will have cast a spell on it to prevent it from being taken!"

Morag looked at him, shocked. She had almost touched it!

"How astute," said a voice behind them. And someone clapped slowly. They spun round to see who had spoken. There in the doorway stood the willowy figure of Mephista, looking a little bemused by the whole situation.

"The bird is quite right," she said. "The stone is protected by a strong spell that only I and my father can break."

She strode into the room, smiling slyly at the stunned group of friends. "Surprised to see me?" she asked, looking from one to another. "Thought I was sleeping like the rest of them? Hmmmmm?" She smiled serenely. "Clever plan, that, putting a sleeping potion in the soup. It had one tiny flaw, though."

She paused dramatically.

"In my position one has to be suspicious. Just like my

father, I have tasters try everything I'm served before I touch it. You can imagine my surprise when I found them all falling asleep at my table. At first, I couldn't understand it, and then it dawned on me that this coincided with the arrival of a group of strangers. I knew then that someone must be after the stone."

Nobody said a word.

"Now!" Mephista snarled, making poor Aldiss and Bertie jump. "What shall I do with you? A traveling minstrel indeed! Colluding with a little servant girl who ought to know better. You're obviously here to steal the stone, and I can't have that now, can I? The Eye belongs to my father."

"That's a lie!" said Bertie. "The stone belongs to Marnoch Mor!"

Mephista gave the little dodo a look that was so evil it made him shriek with fright. Bertie shrank back from her, whimpering. Mephista said nothing, merely slipped her hand into her sleeve and pulled out something long and silvery. She held it up. The wand glittered in the light of the Eye of Lornish. Without taking her eyes of Bertie, Mephista began to chant something under her breath. Everyone watched in terror, rooted to the spot, as Devlish's daughter recited a spell.

"Run!" Morag screamed as Mephista raised the wand higher. Everyone began to run about the circular room looking for an escape route, but there was none except for the doorway that Mephista's tall frame was blocking.

The Lady, deep in the casting of her spell, raised her

arms skyward and then with a loud shout, brought the wand down to point at Bertie. The bird squawked and tried to run behind the Eye, but he wasn't quick enough. A bolt of lightning shot out of the wand and seared the dodo's little feathery tail. With a shriek that could have woken the dead, Bertie jumped high into the air. He landed with a bump, got to his feet and, screaming loudly, ran round and round the room, his rear on fire.

Morag saw what was happening and quickly acted. She pounced on the dodo and began to pat out the flames with her bare hands. Oblivious to the burning heat, she smacked at the tail until there was only a little wisp of smoke coming from Bertie's rump. The dodo looked around at his backside and burst into tears. What had once been soft white plumage was now a stump of smoldering feathers. Morag put her arms around his shivering shoulders.

"There, there, it'll grow back," she assured him, but the little gray bird could not be consoled and wailed all the louder.

Mephista cackled at what she had done and threw her head back. She gave a cruel, mocking laugh that caused her long red hair to shake and shimmer in the light.

"I haven't had so much fun for ages!" she cried. "Now, who's next?" She scanned the room, looking from the dragon to the man to the rat to the little girl. One of *her* maids had been helping these creatures? One of *her* employees? Mephista's face contorted into a vicious snarl.

As Mephista raised her wand again, Kyle and Aldiss ran toward Morag, but Mephista was too quick for them. She realized what they were doing and, using her wand, created an invisible rope that rapidly bound them so tightly that the pair could hardly breathe. Despite their best efforts, they could not wriggle free. They shouted at Mephista to let them go. Instead, she shut them up with a Quieting Spell, which stopped the words in their throats. No matter how much Kyle and Aldiss shouted and screamed, no words came out of their mouths.

Now Shona, on seeing what had happened to her friends, began to growl and snap.

Snarling, the dragon moved slowly toward the witch, like a cat about to pounce on its prey. Instead of worrying Mephista, however, Shona's growling made the witch laugh all the more. With a flick of her wand, the dragon was lifted so high into the air that her great green head bumped against the wooden ceiling. Another flick brought Shona hurtling to the ground. The dragon was winded, but not out, and she got to her feet again and snarled all the more. Casually Mephista threw her up and down a few more times to teach her a lesson. She brought the dragon down with such force that soon poor Shona was knocked out cold.

A horrified Morag could only watch what was happening from her spot on the floor beside the quivering Bertie. She was unable to move, her legs felt like jelly and her throat was dry. She couldn't even feel her hands, which were beginning to smart from the slight burns she had suffered while smothering the flames on Bertie's tail. All she could do was look at Mephista and the wand, mesmerized by the beauty of both. It was Henry, hidden away under her clothes, who suddenly brought her back to reality.

"Get the Eye!" he urged. "Morag! Snap out of it, girl! Go and get the Eye, it's the only way to defeat her!"

"What?" Morag woke from her dreamlike state. She felt for the pendant around her neck. She had become so used to the weight of the great gold medallion that she had forgotten all about him.

"I said get the Eye, it will defeat her," Henry assured her. "Go for the Eye."

"I, I can't!" whispered Morag. "The spell!"

"Don't worry about that," he promised. "I'll think of something."

"And Mephista?"

"I'll deal with her."

"How are you going to do that?" Morag asked.

"Pull me from out of your clothes, I need to be seen by her," the medallion said. "She won't touch you while you are wearing me."

Morag did as she was asked. She pulled Henry from underneath her uniform. The gold caught the light and glinted brightly. Mephista saw it, and frowned, and then seemed to dismiss any concerns she might have and raised the wand again.

"Now, Morag, now!" shouted Henry.

Morag launched into action. She sprang to her feet and leapt over to the Eye. Mephista began to chant once more. The wand in her hand buzzed and crackled. It was building up the energy to strike once more. Morag ran to the Eye and stood before its dazzling brightness. She reached a hand up to grab the giant stone.

"STOP!" warned Mephista. "YOU SHALL NOT HAVE THE EYE!" she screamed. "YOU SHALL NOT HAVE THE EYE!"

Morag dared not look at her. She focused on the Eye at the top of the large wooden staff floating in the middle of the room. She tried to reach the stone, but it was too high up. She jumped to try to grab it, but missed.

"YOU ... SHALL ... NOT ... HAVE ... THE ... EYYYYYYYYEEEEE!" shrieked the she-witch as she precisely aimed the wand at Morag.

A thunderous bolt of dark energy shot in a blast of ferocious sparks toward the girl as she reached out for the Eye. Morag turned round. Her eyes widened with terror as she saw it slice through the air toward her. She heard Mephista utter the words of her enchantment, but it was too late for her to dive for cover. She gritted her teeth, closed her eyes tight and prayed for a miracle.

There was a deafening roar and the room seemed to tear apart. The floor and the walls of the tower shuddered with the force of the blast, throwing Morag to the ground. She felt the pain of her knees hitting the wooden floor and the whack of the staff as it came tumbling down on top of her along with the Eye. Winded, she sat up quickly and looked around. She was a little dazed, but in front of her, smoking and singed, was a shocked Mephista.

The witch still had her wand raised as if to strike again, but only a stub of the magical instrument had survived.

Mephista, her magnificent dress now in tatters and her beautiful hair disheveled, was breathing heavily. Then, with a sigh, she sank to the ground and passed out.

Nearby, Shona was groaning slightly and holding her head. Kyle and Aldiss somehow had been freed from their magical bonds and were crawling across the floor to Shona. To Morag's right, Bertie was getting to his feet. And in front of her, within grasping distance, lay the majestic Eye of Lornish. It had tumbled from the staff as the wooden rod fell, and was lying like a large glowing pebble on the floor. In an instant Morag reached out and picked it up.

"What happened?" asked Bertie, looking a little confused.

"I don't know," replied Morag.

"Mmmm," a little voice groaned. Morag looked down. Henry was moaning quietly to himself.

"That wand was more powerful than I thought it would be," he said weakly.

Morag reached up and took him from around her neck. She held him up to her face. He felt hot, almost too hot to touch.

"Are you all right?" she asked.

"Told you I'd deal with her," he said a little smugly. He winced. "Ow! I hurt all over," he complained. "That's the last time I take on a wand, I tell you."

"You? You stopped her? How?" Morag asked, grateful to the little medallion. She had been sure that the moment before the explosion was going to be her last.

"Who else? I threw up a protective orb around us. It

takes more power than I thought I had, but you're safe. And there's another good thing too," Henry said proudly. "It looks like the blast broke the spell around the Eye."

"Oh thank you, thank you," gushed Morag, kissing the medallion all over.

"Gerroff me!" he yelled. "Gerroff! I can't stand open displays of affection!"

"Sorry!" Morag laughed.

"I hate to break up the party," said Kyle. "But is everyone all right?"

Everyone nodded. They each had their battle wounds, but no one felt the need to complain.

"Then I think we should leave before Her Ladyship over there wakes up," he said, nodding toward the unconscious Mephista. They helped each other to their feet and hurried to the door. Kyle stopped.

"The Eye! We forgot the Eye!" he said in a panic. Morag held it up above her head. "Good work, squirt! Now c'mon, let's get out of here."

With Morag holding Henry and the Eye, Kyle carrying Aldiss, and Shona holding Bertie, one after the other, they ran, jumped and hopped down the spiral staircase. Step after step after step, past sleeping guard after sleeping guard.

After what seemed like an age, breathless and excited, they finally reached the bottom. Shona heaved the door open and a blast of crisp sea air swept in. One by one they ran out into the torchlit courtyard.

It was beginning to rain, icicle-cold droplets of water

speared them, but it did nothing to dampen their high spirits. They had actually pulled it off! Morag and Henry were free and the Eye had been rescued. Still cautious, they took their time sneaking across the shadow-filled courtyard, knowing that the sleeping potion might at any time wear off and the guards might waken. But they needn't have worried: the castle remained sleeping; there was not a soul in sight.

Kyle led the way to the castle gates. With Shona he hauled them open and ushered the others through into the cold winter's night. At the bottom of the hill, in a bay of black sea, bobbed the safety of the fishing boat.

All the way down to the torch-lit jetty, Aldiss could not help chattering excitedly about what had happened.

"Oh, it was marvelous how Morag and Henry saved the day!" he squealed. "We'll all get a medal for sure for this one!"

"A medal, dear boy?" Bertie asked. "Even Henry?"

"Well, he should get the biggest one of all," said the rat. "Because he stopped Mephista in her tracks."

"Are you sure Henry would want a medal?" Bertie asked.

"Oh yes," said Aldiss. "He couldn't refuse. He's a hero."

"Think about it, old friend," said Bertie. "Henry wearing a medal?"

"Uh-huh," said Aldiss, a little miffed that his friend was pooh-poohing his idea. "And what's wrong with that?" he added huffily.

"A medallion being presented with a medal? What do *you* think?" said Bertie with a cackle.

Aldiss paused. "Oh!" he said. "I hadn't thought about it like that! It's ridiculous, of course."

His little brown face screwed up into a thinking frown. "Well, they'll just have to come up with something else for him, but *I'd* still like a medal. I think it would look very nice sitting here," he said, patting his chest.

The friends hurried down to where the little fishing boat was moored. Now there was no one to stop them, and when they finally ran across the jetty they could no longer contain their delight. Even Kyle began to relax a little, enough for him to ask after Shona's health. The dragon told him that her head hurt, but that otherwise she was fine.

"That's good," he replied. "I'm glad you're not hurt. You took some beating."

Shona was about to reply when a flash above the faint line of the horizon caught her eye. Something was traveling at incredible speed toward the island, something black against the brightness of the moonlit sky. She squinted to see what it was. It looked very like a large cloud of migrating birds, but most birds don't fly at night.

"Kyle?"

"Uh-huh?" he answered, half listening.

"What do you think *that* is?" she said, pointing up to the sky with a claw. The dark moving mass was nearly above them.

"I don't know," he said urgently, "but I think we should all get out of here as quickly as possible!"

He grabbed Bertie and lobbed him on board. The bird squawked in shock as his burnt rear banged off the boat's deck. Aldiss followed quickly after him in the same way and landed in a roll at the dodo's feet. Shona climbed aboard, and the little boat rocked dangerously with her weight. All the time, Kyle and Morag were craning their necks up at the sky above them.

"What is it?" asked Morag uncertainly. "It could almost be bats. . . ."

Kyle squinted at the dark cloud that billowed overhead. Sure enough, it *was* a vast cloud of bats. As they got closer, he saw that each one wore a ring around its neck, and connected to the ring was a long thin metal cable. Behind them, held up by the wing power of thousands of squalling, shrieking bats, sailed an immense black gondola gleaming in the moonlight. And at the prow, which was carved into the form of a serpent baring its fangs, was the most terrifying sight any of them had ever seen. A tall man, thin, with a thunderous expression on his pallid face and a Klapp demon at his side.

"Devlish!" squawked Bertie as the gondola started its rapid descent to the shore.

"Quickly!" shouted Kyle over the noise of thousands of shrieking bats. "Morag, get on board!"

But it was too late. Devlish's carriage settled at the foot of the grassy slope. The chattering and screeching of bats drowned out all other sounds, and the winds from the million wing beats furiously chopped the air.

Devlish rose to greet them, his wand drawn.

19

"Going somewhere?" Devlish asked with a sneer as he stepped down from the gondola. The Klapp demon, Percolator, like all Klapp demons, was too cowardly to stand with its master, and cowered at the vessel's prow.

Devlish was a gaunt figure, with an emaciated white face and short hair that was flame red in color, like his daughter's. He wore deep blue robes that denoted his status as a senior male witch and a large golden medallion hung around his neck that was identical to the one Morag was wearing (a fact not lost on her as she glanced down at Henry). Something of Devlish's wickedness showed in the features of his face. He had a long pointed nose with a high bridge, small mean-spirited eyes and thin, pale lips. Lit by the torchlight, his face registered disgust at the man and the girl before him.

No one said a word.

"Was my question too difficult?" he said quietly. "I can answer for you. Firstly, you're going to give me back what is mine and, secondly——" He was interrupted before he could take another breath.

"It's not yours!" said Morag quietly. Devlish glared down at her.

"I don't think you're in any position to tell me what's what, little girl," he said, striding toward her. She did not flinch, but lifted her chin to him in defiance. Suddenly, she didn't feel afraid of anything anymore. She was no longer the weak little prisoner of Moira and Jermy. She and her friends had been through too much to let anyone stop her now, even this warlock of such unimaginable power. *I will not let this happen,* she decided, *not while there is still breath in my body.* She held the Eye tightly in one hand.

"I think I am," she retorted, her eyes full of fire. "I think you'll find that *I* have the Eye and it's up to *me* what happens to it, and I've decided that *I'm* going to do the right thing. I'm taking it back to Marnoch Mor."

Devlish was surprised. No one had ever spoken to him like this before, let alone a little girl. His eyes narrowed in annoyance.

"Don't be stupid, child. Give me the Eye before you anger me further. It will be better for you if you do." He opened his white skeletal hand and held it out for the stone.

Long black nails curled up from the tips of his pointed fingers. Morag shook her head.

"No!" she said simply.

"Give it to me, girl!" Devlish demanded, moving closer to her. His eyes never left hers as he advanced. Morag stepped back. "No!"

"Then I'll take it from you!" He made a grab for her arm, intending to pin the girl down and wrestle the stone out of her grip, but she was too agile for him. She darted away just in time as Devlish's hideous clawing fingers snatched the empty air for her. She ran across the jetty, with the warlock, his face a grimace of fury, at her back.

The wood was slimy and wet, and she found it difficult to keep her footing. At one point she slipped so badly that she tipped forward and nearly fell on her face, but she managed to keep her balance and ran on as Devlish closed in.

Kyle gave chase. He knew he could not let the warlock get to Morag. There was no telling what Devlish would do to her once he caught her.

The girl ran until she reached the very edge of the jetty and there was nowhere else to go. Down below, the cold black water swirled and crashed and Morag fleetingly wondered if this was the very same spot where the servant girl's drowned body had been found. She dismissed the horrible thought from her head and turned to face the advancing warlock. Her heart beating wildly, she looked around for something to protect herself with, but there was nothing.

Seeing he had trapped her, Devlish stopped running and strolled down the wooden walkway. He smiled smugly as he casually approached, his features appearing even more evil in the moonlight. Edging backward, Morag's heels teetered precariously over the edge. Beneath her was nothing but the bitter merciless drop into the icy water.

"Well, well, well, young lady, you are in a bit of a fix, aren't you?" he stated. "How are you going to get out of this one? Hmm?"

Morag did not answer.

"What's wrong? *Rat* got your tongue?" The warlock sniggered. He moved a little closer, and bent down to Morag's height. He shouted at her: "Give me the Eye! Give me the Eye or your friend back there dies!" He pointed to Kyle, who was moving slowly along the jetty toward them. Morag looked to her friend in fear, but again said nothing. Devlish raised his wand and with a small flick launched a tirade of lightning bolts at Kyle. Morag screamed as Kyle dove into the freezing sea below. There was a loud splash and then nothing. Devlish turned his attention back to Morag, a smile playing about his lips.

"Ah, well," he said. "I see your loyalty wasn't strong enough to save him. You've done my work for me. He won't last five minutes in there. And neither will your friends in the boat." He held out his hand again, pointing the wand back at the others. "Or you could stop this. Now give me the Eye!"

"NO!" she shouted, and swung it away from him, losing her footing in the process. She tried to right herself, but had difficulty. If it had not been for the skeletal hand that grabbed the front of her uniform, she would have plummeted into the hungry waves below. Devlish pulled her closer, away from the edge, so close that she could feel his rank, rotten-fish breath on her face.

"What makes you so stubborn, girl?" he whispered. "What did you *lose* for you to hold on to things so tightly?"

Her eyes widened as he moved in.

"Poor lonely child with no one to guide her. Alone in the dangerous world without a mother or father to save her from falling."

He made to shove her over the edge, then yanked her gasping back from the brink.

"Am I correct? Is that what all this is about? You'd give anything for Mummy and Daddy to come home?" His eyes glinted.

"They're lost and calling for you. Can't you hear them? But I can bring them back for you. I can save them if you want me to. And all you have to do is give me what I want. The one little thing that I want and I will make sure you meet your parents again very soon."

Her eyes were large now, and brimming with tears.

"Now, give me what's in your hand," he urged gently. He breathed deeply, sniffing her hair.

Blinking away the tears, Morag took a breath before opening her mouth to speak.

"Devlish, he-witch of Murst," she said in a voice rising from deep within her, "I command you to release me. Let us all go or you *will* be sorry," she continued in as strong a voice as she could muster.

Devlish loosened his grip and stepped back in surprise, giving her enough leeway to pull free. She stood before him, eyes blazing with determination. At first, the warlock seemed a little bemused by her confidence. He had never seen a display like it. Then he burst out laughing, great big hearty chuckles.

"For a moment there I thought you *meant* what you said." He giggled.

"I thought the same about you," she replied.

He laughed harder, wiping tears from his eyes. "Imagine someone as insignificant as you thinking you could defeat me!" He sniggered.

"Not me," said Morag quietly. She held the Eye of Lornish up high. "This!"

The stone glowed brightly in her hand. His laughter stopped and he stared at it in horror.

"Put the Eye down!" he shrieked. "You don't understand its power. Put it down, it's dangerous!"

Morag closed her eyes and began chanting an ancient spell; words that caused the Eye to shimmer and glow white-hot. Devlish looked at her in horror and began to back away. The Eye continued to glow whiter and more brilliantly. Soon it was impossible to look directly at it. Morag continued to hold it up high above her head and chanted louder and louder.

"Dormier . . . actu . . . granssi . . . ," she intoned, her voice rising. Devlish began to back away with haste, his face contorted with fear.

"No! No!" he screamed. "Not that spell! Not that one!"

When Morag opened her eyes, something strange had happened. It was if she had been possessed by the Eye, for her eyes, normally a deep velvety brown, were now a bright glowing white, just like the magical stone itself.

"Meera . . . sanqua . . . seeta . . . GRA!" she screamed.

And Devlish screamed with her. There was a blinding flash of light, and it seemed as if the entire island had been absorbed within the glare. Morag's spell had unleashed the powers of the Eye. The blast that burst forth sent Devlish flying backward. He fell lifeless to the ground, eyes fixed wide in terror and body stiff, as if made of stone. The explosion also caused an immense shock wave to ripple over the immediate vicinity, extinguishing all the torches in one massive gust. The place was plunged into darkness, the only remaining light coming from the full moon.

Morag had been thrown to the floor by the tremor. Despite the violence of the fall, she managed to keep hold of the Eye, preventing it from falling into the sea, from whence it came. She picked herself up from the wet wood of the jetty and dusted herself with her free hand. Dazed, she limped back to Bertie, who had left the boat and was anxiously standing on the shore.

"Oh, Morag, are you all right?" the bird asked, deep concern in his little black eyes. "I thought for a moment there . . . I thought we'd lost you."

"I'm fine," replied Morag. "But what happened?" She looked around her and caught sight of the prone figure of Devlish lying lifelessly nearby.

"Oh! Did I . . . ? Did I kill him?" she whispered, tears in her eyes. Bertie nodded. "And where's Kyle?" she asked, looking around, her voice tight with fear.

"I'm here!" said Kyle as he crawled up onto the beach. He stood up, dripping wet and shivering.

"How did you survive?" asked Morag, happy and astonished.

"I'm a fisherman!" He laughed. "The sea won't take me. Not this time."

"Thank goodness," replied Morag, close to tears at the thought of her friend's dying. "When I saw you go in I thought . . ."

"It takes a lot more than a wee bit of water and a few lightning bolts to get rid of me," he assured her. "Unlike your man over there," he added, pointing to where Devlish lay. Morag burst into tears. Kyle walked up and gave her a wet cuddle.

"Trust me, girl. He deserved everything he got," he said, giving her a squeeze. "Don't you fret about it."

Shona and Aldiss, who had stayed by the boat, paralyzed by fear, joined them. They each, in turn, gave Morag a kiss and a hug. Unsure about what to do next, the friends agreed to leave the body of Devlish where it had fallen. Although no one said it, they were all very relieved to be leaving and they managed to conceal their excitement as they hurried toward the *Sea Kelpie*. They were all dying to ask Morag the same question, but it was Aldiss who eventually plucked up the courage.

"Morag?" he said softly. "How did you do that? How did you know the words?"

"I don't really remember," she replied slowly. "I was holding up the Eye, and after that it's all a bit of a blank. I sort of remember saying things, but I couldn't tell you what I said. It was as if the Eye was talking through me. Does that make sense?"

"Perfect sense," said Bertie. "It's a channel, and very powerful. Perhaps it would be best for me to look after it now?" He held out a wing. "Please give it to me for safekeeping." Morag gladly handed it over. As Bertie took it from her there came an almighty scream from the castle, followed by a prolonged wailing. Morag shuddered. Kyle and the others looked worried.

"I think," he said, "Lady Mephista has just realized we've killed her father. She must have been watching from the tower. Quickly, let's set sail before she comes for her revenge."

The friends broke into a run. Shona led the way, followed by Aldiss and Bertie, then Morag and Kyle brought up the rear. They all jumped back onto the little fishing boat, sending it rocking wildly against the wooden posts of the jetty, where it clunked, metal against wood. Kyle quickly untied the boat and ran to the bridge, where he set the engine roaring. As he did, the rest of the friends turned back to watch the castle fearfully. Every window was lit from within by a ferocious volcanic glare. In the darkness, they could not see very much, but they knew Mephista was coming.

"Hurry, Kyle! Hurry!" Shona called from the stern. The screaming from the castle grew louder and louder, more and more painful, until the friends could hardly bear it. Morag clamped her hands over her ears. The sound was terrible, like a banshee announcing an imminent death. Then suddenly, it stopped.

Kyle reversed the boat just in time. As he spun it backward, they felt the water shudder under the pounding of giant footsteps. In the dullness of the moonlight, they could see hundreds of giant guards filing out of the castle and amassing at the beachhead. A torch flared and was held aloft. The blazing light fell on the cold features of the bearer, and the friends, huddled together on the boat, saw it was Mephista, heading a legion of the beleaguered guards. She appeared to be searching for something. Then she saw it on the shore. Her father's body. The screeching began again, this time more terrible than before.

"They've killed him!" shrieked Mephista. "They've killed my father! You'll pay for this! I will get you! Mark my words! If it's the last thing I do, I will avenge my father's death!"

She continued to scream after them until they could see her and the jagged shoreline of Murst no more. No one spoke until they were far away from the island and the horrible screeching of Mephista had become lost in the wailing of the wind. As the others looked ahead, Morag left her friends and turned back to stare at the dark isle retreating behind them. The darkness seemed to be swallowing up the island. Blinked at once, it looked fainter, Morag thought; blinked at again, the jagged coastline and high towers of the castle were gone and there was only open sea.

They were all exhausted, but too keyed up and excited to sleep. Despite Kyle's best efforts to persuade them to go below and get some rest, they all stayed with him on the bridge until the night started to fade into early morning.

When he noticed Morag huddling against Shona for warmth, he asked Bertie to give her a mug of warm soup from his satchel, and went to fetch a blanket. As he started down the stairwell, he saw that the entranceway and stairs were covered in splintered pieces of wood. He stooped to pick up a mangled hinge, and a few springs and levers that could have once been a lock.

"Tanktop!" he gasped. The battered door hung from its one remaining hinge, and there was a hole where the lock had been clawed out.

Treading carefully so as not to fall and looking around for signs of the enraged demon, he found the cabin empty. But the creature had not left quietly. The remnants of what had once been a door handle, now covered in teeth marks, lay at the foot of the stairs. Kyle's little table where he had enjoyed so many meals had been smashed and thrown into the corner. Plates he had stacked neatly in the little cupboard were in shards on the floor, and the porthole curtains were shredded into dismal tatters. But there was a more horrible fright to come. On the ceiling the Klapp demon had scratched a parting message:

TANKTOP WILL FIND YOU

He thought it best to say nothing when he went back with the blanket to the others on deck. There was no point worrying them unnecessarily. The Klapp demon had gone; that was all he needed to know.

With the soothing hum of the little boat's engine and the soft lapping of the waves to comfort them home, the *Sea Kelpie* rocked gently toward the dawn. The sun was just rising on a gray horizon when they spotted land again.

20

There was a figure in a long flowing robe standing on the pier as they drew closer to Oban Harbor. At first Morag feared that Mephista had somehow beaten them to the mainland, but as they drew nearer, she could see that the figure was not a woman, but a man. His robes were dark in color—blue, Morag guessed—and in his right hand he was holding a tall wooden staff.

As they sailed closer, Morag saw him more clearly and, despite the dimness of the autumn morning, found she could distinguish the features of his face. He was a striking man, with short brown hair, and had a frowning, angry expression. He was scowling as Kyle steered the little fishing boat into the harbor.

"Do you recognize him?" Morag asked Shona. The dragon did not reply, but stood on deck, mouth open. "Aldiss," called Morag. "Who *is* that?"

The little rat, who had been so busy with a biscuit that he had not seen the man on the shore, looked up. His whiskers trembled and straightened out with fright.

"Oh no!" he cried. "I'd better warn Bertie."

"Why? Who is it?" she asked quickly. "Is he one of Mephista's henchmen? Aldiss?"

But the rat was either ignoring her or had not heard, for he bolted in the direction of the bridge, where Bertie was talking to Kyle about the fish in the lochs of Marnoch Mor. At first, the dodo was not too happy about being interrupted, until Aldiss whispered something to him. With a worried look on his face, Bertie excused himself and leapt out of the bridge to flap and hurry to the front of the boat. He squinted in the direction Shona was looking and then, beak open, sat down a bit too quickly on his bandaged tail feathers. It was as if his legs had gone from under him. Morag ran over and knelt by his side.

"Bertie? Bertie? Are you okay?" she asked.

Bertie covered his eyes with one wing and pointed the other at the man on the shore.

"That's . . . That's . . . ," he spluttered. Aldiss filled in the blanks.

"Er, that's Montgomery," he said faintly, positioning himself behind the bird so that he couldn't be seen from shore. "And he doesn't look very happy. Maybe it would be better to turn *back* to Murst. Trust me, Mephista would be easier to face!"

"We can't go back," said Morag. She stood up and looked at the motionless man on the dock. "If it helps, I'll explain everything. I was the one who suggested going to Murst for the Eye. What happened was my fault. I'll tell him that."

Kyle maneuvered the boat alongside the nearest dock post and turned off the engine. He ran out of the bridge and leapt up onto the stone harbor wall. He quickly tied up the fishing boat and looked down at his crew. He had missed all of the talk about Montgomery and couldn't understand why none of his passengers had moved. He looked puzzled.

"You're not telling me you want to go fishing?" he joked. "I thought you'd be glad to get back to dry land."

They looked up at him in silence.

"What's this? Don't tell me you're all under a no-talking spell now?"

"I don't think that's what's making them mute," said a quiet voice behind him. Kyle jumped. He turned round to see standing behind him a man he would later learn was a great and good wizard.

The man put his staff in his left hand and stuck out his right to shake Kyle's hand. "Montgomery—pleased to meet you," he said jovially.

"Kyle," the skipper said, extending his hand. They shook vigorously. Montgomery let go first, leaving Kyle to rub his fingers, sore from the other man's powerful grip.

"Ah, the fisherman?" Montgomery asked. "Yes, I know all about you."

He looked down at the open-mouthed boat passengers below him. "Well?" he said in an imperious tone. "I think you all have a great deal of explaining to do, especially you, Mr. Fluke."

Bertie looked sheepish. "Hello, Your Lordship," he said quietly. "Don't you look well?"

Montgomery ignored him and turned his attention to Aldiss, who was trying to sneak away quietly before he was seen.

"And you, Aldiss Drinkwater," the wizard continued sternly. The little rat froze. "I know you heard me." The rat turned and smiled in the way only rats can smile— showing his big front teeth in a manic grin—and bowed.

"Oh . . . eh . . . hello, Your Lordship," he said nervously. "I didn't see you there. I was just going to . . . em . . . get some cheese, or something."

"You're not going anywhere," Montgomery said slowly. "Until you and your cohorts come ashore and provide me with the very good explanation that I know you must have for this outrageous debacle. Oh, and by the way, did I say 'welcome back' to you, Shona?"

Aldiss looked at Bertie and Bertie looked at Aldiss, and they both looked at Shona. They all had the same realization: they would have to do as they were told. Montgomery was, after all, the world's most powerful wizard. Aldiss helped Bertie to his feet and they began to climb over the boat's railings and onto the harbor's stone walkway. With one finger, Montgomery indicated that Morag, Shona and Kyle should follow too.

In a little harborside café where the magic folk are welcome, Montgomery allowed everyone to settle down and drink their mugs of honeycomb tea and eat toasted cherry blossom bread before he launched into an angry tirade.

"Please enjoy this breakfast with my compliments. For once it's finished, you should all consider yourselves in the severest trouble known to human or elemental."

He seemed genuinely annoyed that they had put themselves in such danger. He turned to Bertie and Aldiss.

"At what point, after you had completed the simple task of freeing Shona, did you feel it was permissible to not only abduct a child from the human world, but to abscond with her to an island prohibited to humans not in the service of Devlish?"

"It wasn't like that," protested Morag. "It's not their fault. I begged them to take me along."

"You may be persuasive, young lady," Montgomery said gravely. "But these two should have known better. What would have happened to the people of Murst if you had been followed? How do we know that there aren't humans drawing up charts of its location as we speak?"

"I know for certain that I wasn't followed," she said.

"Oh? And just how can you be certain?" Montgomery said quizzically.

"No one cares enough to look for me," she replied simply.

Montgomery paused for a moment.

"Well, for another thing, using an enchanted sleeping potion without proper training or a license," he told them, "is against the Witching and Wizarding Rules and is simply not on!"

He was especially concerned, he said, about the approaching repercussions of the "assassination," as he called it, of Devlish. Everyone sat quietly as the senior wizard ranted, and poor Morag, who was still feeling guilty, came close to tears. They all wondered how he knew so much about what had happened to them.

When he finished, Montgomery shook his head, took a deep breath and sipped some tea.

"Furthermore and most importantly," he added a bit more serenely than before, "*I'll* take possession of the Eye, if you don't mind." He held out his hand. Bertie stuck a wing into his satchel and pulled out the stone. It was glowing faintly and looked beautiful even against the checked tablecloth in the cold morning light of the café. Montgomery barely looked at it. He snatched it and stuffed it up the sleeve of his robe.

"I've never heard anything like it in all my years. A motley crew cavorting around the coast with one of our greatest treasures, without a thought for their own or anyone else's safety! What if the Eye of Lornish had been damaged? Or lost? It's unthinkable!"

He turned his attention back to Morag.

"My dear," he said a little more kindly. Noticing her damp eyes, he passed her a handkerchief. "I am so sorry that these fools of feather and fur"—he nodded toward

Bertie and Aldiss, who were squirming in their chairs—
"involved you in this terribly dangerous situation, especially given that they let the Eye use you as a channel to
destroy Devlish. This stone has a power greater than any of
us understand."

"Is that what happened?" mused Shona incredulously.
"We wondered."

"Oh, did you indeed?" Montgomery went on.
"Madame Dragon, is your brain still brick dust? Did you
wonder, by any chance, what would happen afterward
when a human child took information about us back to her
own world, hmm? We could be inundated with estate
agents and zookeepers with tape measures and cages."

The dragon exchanged glances with Bertie and
Aldiss.

"You see, the problems have really only just begun."
Montgomery turned back to Morag, who tearfully looked
away, out the café window to the indistinct horizon, remembering that secret island beyond.

"I'm sorry, it is simply too dangerous for a human child
to know so much about our world and go back to her own.
The human world would soon know about the Underground railway, about Murst and how to find it, and especially about Marnoch Mor, and it would only be a matter of
time before all of it was threatened. And for you to have
been so involved in the bad side of it as well! Oh," he said,
and put his head in his hands, "I don't know what I'm going
to do with you now."

"What do you mean?" asked Morag, suddenly fearful

that Montgomery meant to return her to Jermy and Moira. She'd rather die than let that happen.

"What I mean is that I can't let you go. It would be too dangerous for us," replied Montgomery. "And at the moment, it's too dangerous to leave you here. Mephista will be baying for revenge. She's certainly not going to let *you* escape."

He sat back in his chair and stroked his chin thoughtfully. "Yes, I think it would be best if you came back with us to Marnoch Mor—at least until it's safe again for you to return to the world of humans."

Morag clapped her hands in glee and laughed, suddenly with happy relief. It was not just that she would be living amongst magic folk—real, live magic folk, for she had never dreamed such a thing could happen to her—it was that she was going to live there with her friends. She looked round at them all sitting at the table before her, beaming happily.

"And as for you two," said Montgomery sternly, looking from a shame-faced Aldiss to the teary-eyed Bertie. "You went against my direct orders about trying to rescue the stone. You put yourselves, Shona, Morag and Kyle in danger *and* a member of the Convention ended up paying for it with his life." The expression on his face was severe.

"Yes, but . . . ," mumbled Bertie.

"He wasn't a nice member of the Convention," Aldiss tried innocently. "And it wasn't Bertie's fault. It was the Eye. It enchanted Morag and made her say the things she did."

"And, to be fair to Aldiss, he didn't know you hadn't sanctioned the rescue until too late," confessed Bertie. "I told him you had sent us on this mission. I lied, so if you're going to punish anyone, punish me. It was completely my fault."

Montgomery smiled. "I'm not going to punish anyone," he said. "Although I don't condone what you did, you did get the Eye back for us, *and* you freed Shona."

"They did, sir," agreed the dragon. "And I can't tell you how grateful I am to them." She didn't want her new friends to get into trouble on her behalf. It didn't seem fair.

"And strictly speaking," said Montgomery slyly, "it wasn't completely your idea for the mission, either."

"What!" exclaimed Bertie. "What do you mean?"

"Well," the wizard continued, "I myself couldn't do anything openly about Devlish. That would have been ruinous for the Convention and for my reputation, so I may have let you overhear my conversation about the Eye and Devlish in the hope that you would take matters into your own hands. I didn't think you would go quite so far. I only intended you to rescue Shona. When I realized you might go for the Eye, I sent my second-in-command to help you along." He smiled. Everyone turned to Kyle, who looked completely confused.

"Not me," he said, holding up his hands.

"No, it wasn't you," said Montgomery. He held out a hand to Morag. "May I have Henry back now, please."

"*Henry!*" everyone exclaimed in unison.

Morag reluctantly lifted the chain from around her neck

and handed Montgomery the medallion. Henry beamed as he was returned to his rightful place. His gold shone brightly in the dim light. Holding him carefully in his hands, Montgomery caressed the medallion gently before slipping him around his neck.

"Nice to have you back, old man," he said.

"Nice to be back, young boy," replied Henry with a chuckle.

"You mean, *you* sent Henry to help us?" asked Morag incredulously.

"Yes, and he was able to let me know what was happening," Montgomery replied with a satisfied smile. "Proved very useful."

"How did he do it?" Morag asked.

"I am here, you know," said the medallion crossly. "Why are you asking him when you could ask me? I do exist. I am an individual in my own right."

"Sorry, Henry."

"I'm a magic medallion," Henry began. "I was able to send Montgomery messages back by magic—obviously!" he added, making Morag feel a little stupid.

"Of course!" was all she could say.

"Well, I think we've all had enough excitement for now," said Montgomery as he stood up. "I do believe it's time I took you back to Marnoch Mor and a heroes' welcome!"

He led the band of friends outside and walked them up the main street until they were out of the town and close to a large field in which a herd of black and white cows were lazily cropping grass. Ahead, in the middle of the field, sat a silver helicopter. The pilot, who had been sitting on the grass outside reading a newspaper, jumped to attention when he saw them approach. He saluted Montgomery and opened the passenger door for the wizard. Montgomery beckoned for them all to join him.

"What about Shona?" Bertie asked of the dragon, who was too large to get into the helicopter with them.

"I've made a special provision for her," replied Montgomery, nodding to the space behind them. They turned round to see a long black luxury coach with tinted windows parked in the corner of the field. "You won't get there as quickly as us, Shona, but you will arrive in comfort and in style."

"After everything that's happened, the long way round suits me just fine," said the dragon, laughing and galloping happily toward the vehicle. As she reached the door, she turned round and waved to them all before disappearing inside.

Kyle watched them pile into the helicopter and secure their seat belts. Morag was given the seat closest to the window, as she had never flown before and was very excited.

"Are you sure you won't come with us, even for a few days?" Montgomery asked him. "The least we could do is give you a holiday."

"No offense, sir," he said. "But I belong in this world. I'm happy with my life the way it is. I'm going to go back to fishing. It's the only thing I know."

"I understand," said Montgomery, patting Kyle on the

arm. "And it's heartening to know we have friends like you in this world. You're valuable to us. Take care of yourself. Good luck and good fishing!"

"Thanks, I'll do what I can. Take care of yourselves too. And before you go there's just one other thing. . . ."

His change of tone made Montgomery look back at him.

"Morag. You will make sure that someone looks after her?"

Montgomery nodded kindly. "Don't worry. We intend to guard her with our lives."

Once Montgomery was aboard, the pilot secured the doors, climbed into the cockpit and started up the motors.

The downdraft hit the ground, flattening the grass below and sending the cows running. In the high wind, Kyle backed away down the field. He waved enthusiastically.

"Bye, Kyle! Thanks for everything!" shouted Morag, although she knew he could not hear her words over the sound of the huge blades rotating above their heads. The helicopter rose and turned and they began to fly north.

"You know, I think I could do all that again!" said Aldiss.

"Well, someone else can help you with the map-reading!" laughed Bertie. "Don't you think, Morag?"

She was holding the book her parents had left with her. "Please turn the helicopter around," she said suddenly. "And take me back. I've just realized. I can't go to Marnoch Mor."

"Of course you can, you'll like it there," replied Bertie. "And you belong there now."

"You know how much it would mean to me, but what about my parents?" she cried, starting to panic. "How will they find me if I'm not even in this world? They'll be knocking on doors for me in the real world and they'll never find me there! I'll be even more lost in Marnoch Mor than I was with Jermy and Moira!"

"Shush now," said the dodo softly. "You have to trust that parents have their ways."

"Think of it this way, child. They made you resourceful," said Montgomery from behind them. "They made you brave. And even the smallest courage can change the world. That part of them is still with you, so in some ways they've never really left you. And that's not so bad, is it?"

"I suppose not," said Morag, sniffing.

"Just look ahead," said Aldiss.

"That's very wise for such a little rat," commented Bertie.

"No, I mean there it is, straight ahead—Marnoch Mor!"

Morag sat bolt upright in her seat and peered out the helicopter window. An unfamiliar feeling of warmth and security was spreading through her body. For the first time in her life she felt that things might turn out well, now she had proven to herself that she had it within her to do good things and be happy. She smiled. Maybe this is the start of good things happening to me, she thought, hugging her book.

The sky was clearing, and long shafts of sunlight dropped through the clouds and passed over the forests and hillsides, lighting the great lochs and plains below. And there she saw, on the distant horizon, silhouetted against the sky like a bank of clouds, the spires and mountains of that strange place where dodos and dragons still live, and where lost children are lost no more.

D. A. NELSON was born in Glasgow and lives in Cardross, Scotland. She was a journalist for many years before moving into public relations. She started writing at an early age and still has a pile of stories she wrote as a child. She loves books, and her favorite pastime is sitting in a bookstore, cup of tea and muffin in hand, reading a fantastic new novel.

DarkIsle was inspired by a sculpture of a huge stone dragon created by Roy Fitzsimmons that overlooks Irvine Beach on Scotland's west coast. This is D. A. Nelson's first novel.